Th

& Dirty Holidays

Books 1-4

Celia Aaron

Nicole,

There's nothing with getting filthy at the holidays.

xoxo,

Celia Aaron

The Hard & Dirty Holidays

Celia Aaron

Copyright © 2015 Celia Aaron

All rights reserved. No part of this book may be reproduced, scanned, or distributed in any printed or electronic form without prior written permission from Celia Aaron. Please do not participate in piracy of books or other creative works.

This book is a work of fiction. While reference may be made to actual historical events or existing locations, the names, characters, places and incidents are products of the author's imagination, and any resemblance to actual persons, living or dead, business establishments, events, or locales is entirely coincidental.

WARNING: This book contains sexually explicit scenes and adult language and may be considered offensive to some readers. Please store your books wisely, away from under-aged readers.

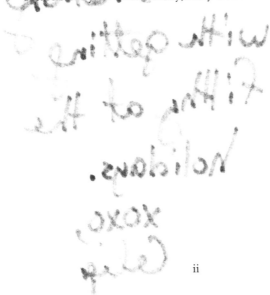

OTHER BOOKS BY CELIA AARON

Counsellor
The Acquisition Series, Book 1

Magnate
The Acquisition Series, Book 2

Sovereign
The Acquisition Series, Book 3

***

Cleat Chaser
Celia Aaron & Sloane Howell

***

The Forced Series
***

Zeus
Taken by Olympus, Book 1

Sign up for my newsletter at AaronErotica.com and be the first to learn about new releases (no spam, just send free stuff and book news.)

Twitter: @aaronerotica

CONTENTS

CELIA AARON

A Stepbrother for Christmas

CHAPTER ONE
ANNALISE

I STOMPED AROUND ON the porch of the chalet. Snow clung to my boots and lay thick and deep on the surrounding slopes. The wind was bitter, slicing through my clothes and stinging my skin. I wasn't dressed for the weather quite yet.

I'd just driven in from the airport. Mom had decided this Christmas would be best spent on the slopes of Aspen instead of in Dallas. I didn't intend to come, especially since I had a lot of schoolwork over the Christmas break. This year, though, Mom wouldn't take 'no' for an answer.

Once satisfied I wouldn't leave a cold, wet trail through the rental, I opened the front door and dragged in my suitcase. Mom had gone to the trouble of setting up a Christmas tree, presents scattered at its base and overdone ornaments and ribbons choking whatever green was on its branches.

The chalet was homey, wooden beams and glass mixing to give an earthy and airy feel. The front windows gave a great view of the mountain and the town.

"Mom!" I called.

My stepfather, Brent, came around the corner and

greeted me. "Annalise, my darling, how good to see you." He gave me a warm hug, going on and on in his posh British accent about how much he'd missed me.

I'd always liked Brent. He'd married my mother five years prior. He was a great stepdad, caring and warm. He'd helped me make it through some tough times in high school and then again in college. He was handsome for his age and well respected in his professional community. My mom had definitely picked a good one – especially when compared with my absentee biological dad.

For all the good things Brent was, he only had one fault. It wasn't a fault, really. He couldn't help it. His son being a total dick wasn't even Brent's doing as far as I could tell. But Niles Tremaine, my stepbrother, was a total asshole. He'd tormented me ever since our parents got married. It was as if he blamed me for his mother's death. He was always nasty to me, humiliating me in front of friends, dates, or anyone standing within a ten-foot radius. I never understood how the kindly Brent spawned such a demon.

The moment I heard Niles was going away to college in Oxford, England, I couldn't be happier. I was able to spend my senior year of high school in peace. Then, thanks to a fortuitous series of events, I hadn't crossed paths with him for the next two years. I still heard all about him, thanks to my mother bragging every chance she got about how he was a scholar at Oxford, on the rowing team, and on and on. I didn't care what his grades were. He was an unrepentant asshole.

"Your mother has really outdone herself this year." Brent waved his hand at the Christmas tree.

"I can see that." I pulled my cap off, letting my dark hair fall freely down my back.

"Anna!" Mom rushed into the room, her usual ball of frenetic energy. Howie, her sheltie, was hot on her heels and barking with excitement. I leaned down to pet him and gave him a few "good boys" as he jumped around excitedly, his nails clicking on the hardwoods. He was getting older, but he was fluffy, fun, and operated under the mistaken belief he was still a small puppy.

When I stood, Mom gave me a full once over. Her eyes were a darker brown than mine, though her black hair was streaked with gray. Even so, she was still a looker. Tall and willowy with a dancer's body. I was a little curvier, but had the height. Despite her grace, she hugged like a bear, and wasted no time crushing me in her embrace.

"Mom. Can't. Breathe."

She loosened up her grip and put her hand on my face. "You're frozen! This isn't Dallas."

"Thanks for the pro tip." I changed the subject before she got stuck on the subject of how I didn't understand thermometers. "Tree looks great."

Her eyes lit up. "You like it?"

"It's beautiful." I wondered if there was an actual tree up under all the garlands and bows.

"Well, Brent helped me quite a bit."

He wrapped an arm around her waist. "I just climbed the ladder around one hundred times or so."

She kissed him on the cheek. "Because you love me."

"That I do." His smile was lopsided and heartfelt.

I realized how much I missed them. School took all my time and I stayed away from the house whenever I heard Niles would be visiting.

Mom and Brent were a cute couple, the cutest really. But I didn't need to be subjected to googoo eyes this early in the visit. I was spending two weeks with them. I tried to cut it to one because I was working on finishing my biology degree early so I could start med school. Mom guilted me into coming for the entire two weeks. She has a gift, that woman.

"I'm just going to go on upstairs."

"I thought you were going to bring Gavin with you?" Brent asked.

Mom elbowed him hard in the ribs.

"Oh, oh too right. I forgot. My apologies, darling. Can I help you upstairs with your bag?" Brent's faced turned an interesting shade of crimson in only seconds.

Gavin was my ex-boyfriend. I'd dated him for a few months before we ended things. He just wasn't the one. I liked him, we had a lot in common, but there was no spark, no fire. It didn't really bother me to talk about it, but talking about my love life – or its untimely death, I supposed – with my parents was not happening.

"Which room is mine?" I clunked the bag up the stairs.

"Second door on the left, next to Niles'."

I stopped, my foot almost missing the stair entirely. "Niles is coming?"

"Oh, he's already here. Went to town to get some supplies, he said," Mom trilled.

I slammed my bag to the top of the stairs, unable to hide my irritation.

Merry Frickin' Christmas.

CHAPTER TWO
NILES

I SWIRLED THE COFFEE around, trying to cool it a bit before taking a sip. It had been a long trip over the pond, and even longer to get to Colorado. I was looking to relax for a few weeks, do some skiing, see my dad. I was almost finished with university, getting ready to seek a job in finance. I couldn't decide if I wanted to come back to the States to be closer to my dad or stay in England where I'd made so many friends.

The coffeehouse traffic bustled around me, tourists streaming in and out for their coffee fix. The barista gave me a smile. She'd slipped me her number along with my coffee. She was certainly pretty enough, but I wasn't here for a fling. I'd done enough of those at Oxford to last a lifetime. I smiled back at her before dropping my eyes. No point being rude.

The door opened with a jingling sound accompanied by a woman with a scarf, hat, and sunglasses. She was curvy and tall. I couldn't quite see her face, but it had to be gorgeous like the rest of her. I straightened in my chair and ran a hand through my auburn locks, smoothing them down as best I could.

She shifted from one foot to the next as she waited to order. Her ass, a perfect plump orb, moved in her jeans. She had a small waist and her tits were high and large. My cock hardened in my pants as any number of inappropriate thoughts rushed through my mind. I licked my lips as heat rose along my skin.

She ordered her drink, a dizzying combination of flavors that I couldn't follow, and turned toward the area where I sat. When she saw me she stiffened and reached for her sunglasses. She pulled them off and gave me a look that could melt lead.

Bloody hell. "Annalise?"

"Niles." She moved away toward the bar area. To the barista, she said, "I need that in a to go cup, please. As soon as possible."

Clearly, she'd wanted to sit in the shop for a while, but my mere presence was about to drive her back out into the cold again. I couldn't blame her. I'd been a total wanker to her the entire time I'd lived with her and her mom in Dallas. I was in a bad head space at that time in my life. My mom had died two years before. I couldn't forgive my father for remarrying. I took it out on Annalise. I knew that now. I'd thought so many times about how I might try to apologize, to make it up to her. But we were strangers now, more or less, and I didn't want to reopen old wounds.

By the way she cringed away from me in the coffee shop, it appeared the wounds had never fully closed. And going three years without an apology from me? I was the biggest tosser this side of the Atlantic.

I stood and took a step toward her. She leaned away even though I was several meters from her. This was going to be slow going. Getting closer to her was clearly not an option. I resume my seat. She eyed me like I was a particularly loathsome rodent. I rubbed my hand over my jaw, desperately trying to figure out how to rectify a five-year mistake in five minutes over coffee.

When her order was up she thanked the pretty barista and took her drink. She gave me one more acidic glance and headed toward the door.

"Annalise," I called.

She stopped.

"Please, I just want to talk is all." I tried to give her my most winning smile.

She grimaced.

Fail.

The barista watched the scene with interest. She perked up at my accent. All the American women did. Except Annalise.

She seemed caught in a fight or flight instinct. *Was I really that bad?*

One look in her eyes told me yes, I really was.

"Please?" I dropped the smile and just tried to straight up grovel.

She relaxed a bit, her stance not quite as tense. The door opened, sending a blast of cold air onto her. She shied away from the chill, back toward the dining area. Back toward me.

She squared her shoulders, as if she were about to take on an entire rugby team, and approached. The frown on her face told me I was barely the winner in the Niles versus hypothermia battle.

She eased into the chair opposite me and continued her skeptical perusal.

"You've gotten big."

She arched an eyebrow.

Good one, Niles.

"I mean, you've grown. Not that I'm saying you've grown like big. I mean, like, you've filled out and ..." *Stop, just stop talking.*

She crossed her arms over her chest, which only made her breasts look bigger. *Mayday, mayday.*

I took a gulp of my too-hot coffee to avoid having to make any more sounds with my mouth. It burned like the

7

fires of hell, but I didn't make a peep. Christmas music piped through the speakers and did a poor job of covering the uncomfortable silence.

She'd sat with me. It would have to be enough. Besides, just busting out an apology with no explanation or build up didn't seem to be the best move. Or did it? I couldn't tell. All I knew was she was giving me a death glare I wasn't sure I'd ever recover from.

She took a small sip of her coffee and her gaze slid to the door. I was losing her. I couldn't stall. It was now or never.

"I'm sorry."

Her eyes opened wide and she set her coffee down so hard it geysered from the lid and landed with a slap in the floor.

"Sorry?" she hissed. "Sorry for tormenting me, calling me names, embarrassing me, spreading lies about me at school, getting other kids to call me 'assless Anna'? I could go on, *Niles*." She put a lethal dose of venom into my name.

She was right. I had been a rotten prick to her.

"I know. And you're right to be angry." I didn't think she'd still be *this* angry, but I supposed what I thought didn't matter at this point. "I was having a hard time with our parents' marriage and I did and said things I never should have. I've wanted to apologize—"

The pretty barista came up and bent over to clean the spill. Her ass was in the air, her magenta thong clearly visible over the top of her jeans. I glanced away from it, but it was too late. Annalise had seen me looking.

"You can't be serious right now." Her voice rose, anger in each note. "You want me to come over here and sit while you try to explain how sorry you are for torturing me when we were teenagers and, just to put the cherry on top, you ogle the waitress? You think this is a joke? You think those years of you treating me like an ugly stepsister were funny?"

"Hey, I'm a barista, not a waitress." Pretty barista really didn't need to interject herself.

Annalise threw her hands up. "You know what? I'm done." She grabbed her coffee and practically darted to the door. She looked back once. I don't know why. But I saw the tears gleaming in her eyes and it tore at my heart. Then she was gone out into the cold.

CHAPTER THREE
ANNALISE

I STUMBLED OUT OF the coffee shop, painful memories swirling through my mind. I thought I'd gotten over all of it, all of the horrible things Niles had said and done. I had no idea just seeing him would cause it all to come bubbling back to the surface. It didn't help that when I first glanced at him, I thought he was a ridiculously handsome stranger. Then I realized it was *him*.

Having to sit with him and listen to him tell me how he was sorry? It was torture even if it was delivered in a posh accent.

I rushed to the street corner and waited for the light. Cars with red reindeer noses drove by on the slushy street. The chalet was a few blocks away. I couldn't get there fast enough. It was freezing and I was desperate to lock myself in my room and calm down from the pain Niles inflicted. Just like old times.

I took a swig of coffee, desperately trying not to make a mess as my hands shook. The light finally turned and I crossed the street. I crunched through the gray snow and up onto the opposite curb. Then I struck up a quick stride, fighting against the sting of the wind. But compacted snow

11

must have stuck to the soles of my flats, because one foot skidded out from under me and I was falling. I squeaked as both feet lost purchase.

Strong arms wrapped around me and put me back on my feet. I steadied myself and looked up at my savior. Bright blue eyes, square jaw, red hair – Niles.

"Thought you could use a little help." His hand was still on my elbow, sending heat through the joint and up my arm. Something was in his eyes I'd never seen before. Warmth.

I shook my head. Three years couldn't turn Satan to a saint. It was the same old Niles. I yanked my elbow away.

"Thank you. I can handle it from here." I turned my back and kept walking.

I made it the next corner and waited on the light. He was behind me. I could feel him, as if the air between us was expanding and buffeting against me like a strong wind. I shot him a sharp look over my shoulder.

He shrugged. "We're going to the same place."

The sparkle in his eye was irritating. Yes, only irritating, nothing more. I turned back around and crossed with the light. He maintained a steady pace behind me, never coming to walk by my side. *Good.*

I reached the next corner and paused while other people crossed or waited for the light at the busy intersection. They were buzzing about Christmas shopping, lift passes, and skiing gear. All I could focus on was him. He edged closer as more people gathered at the corner. I scooted up closer to the curb. Traffic had ebbed and I wanted to cross, the light be damned.

Before I could step into the street, he put a hand on my waist and pulled me back. "Wait for the light."

A car turned right in front of us. It would have hit me if I'd stepped down like I'd intended.

Damn. Niles was throwing off my headspace, making me do things that were beyond dumb.

I just needed to get to some sort of sanctuary where I

could think straight. His hand was still on my waist, making any rational thought impossible. My hair stirred at my ear from his warm breath, scented with delicious coffee. His fingers pressed into me almost possessively. His chest was hard against my back as he kept me against him.

"Calm down, Annalise. I'm not going to hurt you. Not anymore." It was a whisper I wanted to believe.

The light finally changed and we were moving. When his hand left my waist, I missed its pressure and warmth. Like an idiot.

The crowd spaced out as we reached the next corner and only a handful kept trudging up the slope along with Niles and me. We passed storefronts with ropes of garland and lights. Scents of peppermint and cinnamon flavored the air. I should have felt comforted. Instead, I felt on edge. My emotions were roiling. Niles didn't seem like the boy I remembered. The one who stole my diary and read my most secret thoughts before throwing them back in my face. Red suffused my face at that particularly painful memory.

Maybe he was different. I granted him that. But would that be enough to make me reconsider anything? *How much could a person really change?*

"Annalise, please, just let me walk with you." He stayed behind me, waiting for my permission. No, definitely not the Niles I remembered. The Niles of days past would have barreled past me, not caring if I fell on my ass. Actually, he would have preferred that outcome.

I slowed my pace. He matched me, still waiting for some sign of assent. I took a deep breath and waved my hand in a "come on" motion. He took the few steps between us and walked at my elbow. We moved along a bit slower than my previously frenzied pace. He smelled wonderful, like coffee and some sort of woodsy soap. I pushed my scarf further up, trying to cover my mouth and nose against the invading scent.

"Cold?"

Was that genuine concern in his voice, his blue eyes? I looked away quickly, staring up toward the chalet. I was frozen, my Dallas wardrobe no match for the mountain winds. But I just wanted to get out for a little walk and a lot of caffeine. A shiver shot through me.

Niles moved closer to my side. "Here." He shrugged off his heavy coat.

"Wait. No." I tried to scoot away. The last thing I wanted was help from Vile Niles. But he slung the warm coat around my shoulders. It was toasty and smelled even more like him. "Won't you freeze."

"No, I'm good. Really." He was wearing a blue plaid button-down with some sort of thermal looking undershirt. His jeans were a dark blue, hitting his muscular frame in all the right places. *Whoa.* That was not the way to be thinking. Not at all.

"So, how's school?" He asked, his elbow touching mine lightly as we ambled past the bustling storefronts.

"Fine." I drew my arm closer. Touching was bad, especially when I couldn't decide if I wanted to run or snuggle more deeply into the coat that smelled like him.

He sighed. "Okay. I get it. Walking's enough for me." He looked down into my eyes. "For now."

A little thrill went up my spine at his words. Disgust, surely that was why.

We walked the rest of the way in silence. Ugly memories paraded through my mind but they were cut off by his hand at the small of my back when we maneuvered around some ice or the way he looked at me with concerned yet somehow hopeful eyes. Confusion settled over me like a fresh snow. I'd always believed that the best predictor of future behavior was past behavior. But Niles was destroying that paradigm moment by moment.

By the time we reached the chalet, the sun was already sinking behind the mountain, sending everything into shadow. The chalet was lit up, warm light pouring out of the wide windows. Mom's Christmas tree glowed through the night, beautiful and overdone at the same time.

"Your mom went all out on the tree." Niles opened the front door for me and stood back so I could pass. *Who is this man?*

"Yeah." I entered the home, the smell of some sort of delicious food, spiced with citrus, hit me in the nose. The uphill walk back to the chalet had made me even hungrier. I stripped off Niles' coat and handed it back to him. He took it and hung it on the pegs by the front door and held his hand out for my light jacket. I pulled it off along with my scarf and hat.

I caught his stare. He'd tensed as I'd removed the knit warmth piece by piece. He watched me intently now, his eyes hungry. I wanted to look away, to forget I saw that look. But I couldn't. My heart pounded and my skin felt as if his hands were on it, touching and teasing. His adam's apple bobbed as he swallowed hard and broke eye contact. He hung everything up and turned back to me, his eyes no longer giving anything away. Guarded.

"Anna?" Mom called.

I let out a breath, not even aware I'd been holding it. "Coming."

I followed her voice through the living area and into the kitchen. Niles followed.

"Oh, there you are. And I see you found Niles." Mom's smile faltered.

"Yes. We got a coffee."

"Together?" Mom flipped a browned fish filet in a pan with an obscene amount of butter. Brent was setting the table in the adjacent dining room.

"Not really." I spotted an open bottle of red and beelined for it.

"With the fish, Anna?" Mom asked. "I thought we'd have a white."

I didn't care what color it was, I just needed alcohol. I poured a glass and took a decidedly unladylike gulp. Mom turned and watched me over her shoulder as she worked on the island cooktop. She raised an eyebrow in question. I shook my head. I couldn't discuss anything right now, especially not with Niles in the room. She took the hint and returned to dinner.

Niles leaned against the door frame, not exactly relaxed. Handsome, though. Too handsome. I took another drink. Undeniably gorgeous. I drained the glass and poured another.

Brent walked past with a bowl of salad. "Go easy, Anna. We have to have enough wine to get sauced every night for two weeks. I'll start rationing if necessary."

I laughed and raised my glass to him. Niles smiled and began helping Brent with the food. Mom bossed me around a bit and we all fell into our roles. I had never been much of a cook, so getting the salad dressing and watching Mom make the risotto was the height of my participation. When it was all done, we sat down and dug in. I was across from Niles and made a point of not looking at him.

"So, Niles, tell us about your rowing team. I heard there was a competition or something that's a big deal in England?" Mom asked.

Brent laughed and shook his head. "It's much, much more than just a competition. The Boat Race is, is—" he leaned back in his chair, eyes misting beneath his glasses "—transcendent. My year with the blues, we beat Cambridge by a full thirty seconds. Thirty seconds, can you believe that? Those were the days, I tell you."

"Blue?" I smiled, my body lighter than it had been all day. "So Oxford team is blue? Is Cambridge red, then?"

"We're both blue, actually," Niles said.

I took another drink of wine. Mom was nuts. This red went perfectly well with the fish she'd made. I giggled. "Both blue? What sort of crap? How do you even tell which team is which?"

"Oxford wears a more dignified darker blue, almost navy. Cambridge, tossers with no sense of style, wear some lighter blue. Hideous, really." Brent took a respectable drink of wine.

Niles nodded in agreement.

"So you won?"

Niles raised his gaze to meet mine. "Yes, my team did."

"Your *team?*" I laughed. "I'm shocked anyone would let you on a team with other normal human beings. Were they afraid you'd kill them in their sleep or something if they didn't?"

The room fell silent and Mom dropped her fork onto her plate with a clink. "Anna! Apologize right this minute."

"I won't. You know what I mean, right Niles?"

He closed his eyes and when he opened them I saw pain there, pain I'd inflicted. I thought it would feel good, hurting him the way he'd hurt me so many times. Instead, I just felt sick.

"Annalise—"

"No, it's okay, Ellen. Really." Niles wiped his mouth and tossed his napkin down next to his half-finished meal. "I need to turn in. It was a long flight and I'm beat. Thanks for this lovely dinner. Delicious as always. Please excuse me." He rose and squeezed his dad's shoulder before leaving.

The room seemed to deflate, as if I'd stuck a pin in it. Mom took what was left of my wine and put it out of my reach.

"Really, Mom?" I rolled my eyes and tamped down my unease. *Was she right?*

"Yes, really Anna. Why would you say something so awful?"

I fisted my hands next to my plate. "Oh, *I'm* awful. Have you forgotten about how he treated me?"

"That was years ago, Anna. You're two different people now, all grown up. It's obvious he's changed and so have you." She neatly folded her napkin and gave me a pointed look. "But I don't know if all of the changes were for the better."

I winced at her words. She was my biggest cheerleader. Her words were a shock to my system. Was I being a jerk? I pushed back from the table.

"Anna, it's okay. Stay—"

"No, Brent. It's fine. I don't want to ruin the rest of the dinner. I'm going to bed. I'll see you two in the morning." I didn't look at Mom as I strode out with angry steps. Petty? Maybe.

The second I was out of the room, they began talking in low voices.

I climbed the stairs, tripping once before I made the landing. Niles' door was closed. I stopped in front of it. Should I apologize? A chant of "assless Anna" ricocheted through my mind from my ninth grade year. No, definitely not apologizing. I went to my room and changed into a t-shirt and panties before going to the bathroom. It was a jack and jill between Niles' room and mine. His door was closed.

A few of his items were on the counter – razor, toothbrush, and the delicious soap I kept smelling. I stilled and tried to listen for him. Nothing. He must have already been asleep. I brushed my teeth, trying not to think about what I'd said earlier. Once I was done in the bathroom, I slipped into the queen size bed. I was beat from the trip and admittedly a little drunk. Sleep took me quickly.

***

A weight settled on me. My eyes flew open. Red hair, blue eyes. Niles had his hand over my mouth.

"Be quiet, Anna. Let's not wake our parents."

Panic rose in my throat, but I didn't make a sound. He removed his hand and stroked through my hair.

"What are you doing?" I hissed.

He leaned in, his lips so close to mine. "I just wanted to apologize and do it right this time."

"You call this doing it *right*?"

He laughed, low and seductive. "I saw the way you looked at me. And I've read your diary, remember? I know this is how you want it."

I drew a hand from under the sheet to slap him but he caught my wrist and pinned it to the bed. My heart pumped double time and my clit began to tingle. He was right. This – what he was doing – was my kryptonite. I'd always had fantasies of being forced. No one had been able to deliver. That's why all my relationships ended. But the fear mixing with exhilaration in my veins told me that Niles could give it to me.

"So let me make it up to you. Let me be your fantasy." He bent his head to my neck and nipped at my skin lightly.

I couldn't tell if I was in a dream or a nightmare. Perhaps a mix of both.

Could I do this? When he fastened his lips to my jugular and sucked, I arched to him. Yes, I could do this. That seemed to be all the answer he needed. He got to his knees and ripped my blankets away. He was shirtless, his tan skin smooth and beautiful in the low light.

Am I insane?

He grabbed my panties, fisting the material in his palm and ripping. I made a surprised sound and he was on top of me again, his hand slapped over my mouth.

"Not a sound," he rasped in my ear.

He reached down with his other hand and before long, I felt his head at my entrance. I was so wet, from the moment I awoke to find him holding me down, to now. The sensation of his tip pushing into my innermost flesh thrilled me more deeply than I thought possible. He took a fistful of my hair in one hand and kept the other clapped over my mouth.

Even in the darkness of the room, I could see the intense look in his eyes. He was a predator and it was time to take what was his. *Holy shit.*

'Scared, little slut?"

I nodded even as my pussy clenched at his dark tone.

"You don't even know scared." He pushed inside me, his hips surging forward.

I cried out against his hand at the quick pain and the flood of pleasure. He gave me only a second to adjust before he was pounding into me, fucking me harder than I'd ever been fucked in my life. I loved every stroke, every impact, every exhale of his breath as I moaned against his hand.

His mouth was at my earlobe, licking and biting. "I know you want this cock. Your slippery little cunt told me so."

He punished me, making my pussy wetter and plumper with his rough treatment. I wrapped my legs around him, digging my heels into his surging back. The pain along my scalp only made everything more real, more blindingly erotic. He bit down on my neck and I shuddered beneath him, pleasure covering my senses like a net.

My hips were already seizing, getting closer and closer to the ecstasy his body promised. With each hard stroke, he jarred my clit further and further toward the edge.

"Are you going to come, slut?"

His dirty talk caused a sensory overload. My moans into his hand intensified as my throbbing pussy made it clear I was on the verge of sweet release. I had never gotten so high so fast before. He was like a shot of adrenaline, waking my body up from a long sleep.

He locked eyes with mine, owning my body, my mind. His jaw was tense, his eyes fierce.

"Fucking. Hot. Cunt." He punctuated each word with an even harder stroke.

I froze, my body seizing as my pussy contracted and spasmed, holding onto his cock as he continued his punishing pace.

"That's right. Come for me," he grated into my ear. Then he grunted, low and masculine. His cock kicked inside me and he shoved as deep as he could. He gave a few more smooth strokes before pulling his hand from my mouth.

I gasped in deep gulps of air as he collapsed on top of

me, his cock still embedded in my pussy.

"Holy shite, Anna."

"Oh my god. Oh. My. God." It was all I could say, all I could think. I was suddenly religious after his cock showed me the light.

He dropped kisses along the spots where he'd bitten me earlier. "I'm afraid I've left a few marks."

His mouth was delicious on my stinging skin. He met my eyes, the predatory gaze gone. He was soft now, caring – more so than he'd ever been when we were younger.

"Are you okay? I didn't hurt you, did I?"

Oh, yes. Yes, you did. In the best possible way. "No. I'm fine. Really. That was just so…"

What was it? I didn't quite have a metaphor for what being rough fucked by your loathsome stepbrother was truly like.

"I know." He brushed his lips over mine so softly – our first real kiss.

Then he rose. When his cock slid out, a frustrated sound caught in my throat.

"More, Anna?" He laughed, low and sensual. "Don't get greedy on me. I have two weeks to make it all up to you."

He pulled his pajama pants up and backed off the bed.

In the low light he looked like a dark sex god, one that could make my deepest desires come true. Hadn't he?

He disappeared into the bathroom and clicked his door closed with a quietly called "goodnight."

CHAPTER FOUR
NILES

MY HEART RACED AS I lay back down. Her scent was still on my body, and I knew it would color my dreams with her. Of all the things I'd done in my life, creeping into her room was by far the ballsiest. My cock hardened just remembering how she looked when she was asleep. Her large breasts strained against the fabric of her t-shirt and her dark hair streamed next to her on the pillow. She was gorgeous, far more beautiful than I remembered.

I strummed my fingers across my chest. What did I remember? I remembered being a total tool to her. She was right. Everything she felt or thought about me came from experience and I couldn't blame her for it. But then she'd let me take her somewhere I could tell she'd never been before.

The words from her diary came piling into my mind as I'd lain awake and listened to her get ready for bed.

I had my first time last night with Gill. It was short, but he tried to be sweet about it.

Gill and I had another fight. He wanted to do it again, but I asked him to do what I wanted. Pull my hair. Do it really hard. Make it feel like he was taking something from me. He freaked out.

Gill and I broke up. He said I was sick for wanting what I wanted. He said I'd never find a man who would treat me like that short of bondage freaks.

If I knew where Gill lived, I would have been more than happy to go there and beat him senseless for touching her, for starters. For finishers, I would stomp the shit out of him for making her feel like anything other than the amazing woman she was. But who was I to do any of that? I had no doubt I'd made Anna feel worse about herself than Gill ever could.

I turned over on my side and stared out the window at the falling snow and the all-encompassing darkness. I closed my eyes, her beautiful body imprinted on the insides of my eyelids. I couldn't erase the past, but I could make it up to her in the present.

***

I'd slept better than I had in months. I dressed and went down to breakfast.

I took a deep breath and went into the kitchen. I didn't know what to expect. My palms were damp and I wished I'd checked to see if Annalise was still in her room. Her door was closed, though, and I wasn't sure if I'd be welcome.

Howie sat in the doorway, blocking my path and demanding attention. I had to give it to him. He was a great dog – smart and loyal. I scratched his head and let him give me a few good licks on the cheek. Once satisfied, he trotted into the kitchen to look for any surprise human food that may have been dropped.

I followed to find Ellen, Dad, and Annalise all talking and laughing as Annalise tried to make pancakes. I winced at her technique. The finished product would definitely be crunchy given the amount of egg shell she was dripping into the batter.

When she noticed me, she looked up and pink spread along her cheeks. She looked like a winter wet dream. Long dark hair free down her back and her body encased in warm, white layers—form-fitting pants with a fleece top and a turtleneck beneath it. I was glad she thought to hide the marks on her neck. It might be difficult to explain to our parents how she managed to get a set of love bites overnight.

My heart sped up and banged against my ribs as she smiled at me. It was somehow shy despite what we'd shared the night before. Beautiful beyond belief, all the same.

Ellen cleared her throat and I realized I'd been gawking for an awkward amount of time.

I recovered under Ellen's gaze. "So, what's for breakfast?"

"Anna is cooking some delicious pancakes. Quite fabulous, no doubt." Dad winked at me.

"Looking forward to it. Can I help?"

"Go ahead and set the table." Ellen looked between me and Anna, as if unsure whether we would start sparring again.

It depended on Annalise. Her beautiful smile told me one thing, but I didn't know if her mouth would tell me another. After all, it was only one night and I had years and years to make up for. The thought made me grin.

"What's gotten into you this morning?" Dad clapped me on the back and sank into his chair.

"Just glad to be back Stateside I guess."

"It grows on you, doesn't it? I don't miss much – maybe hot cross buns and tea time – but this—" he waved his hand toward the women in the kitchen "—is far better than anything I could have ever imagined. Worth it, yeah?"

For the first time, I actually agreed with him on the point. One glance back at the snow white dream in the kitchen cemented it. I was happy to be back, and the reason was making a mess of pancake batter.

"Yeah." I sat down and watched Ellen try, and fail, to teach Annalise how to prepare breakfast. Ellen eventually took over and Annalise came and sat at the table with us.

She tucked a dark lock behind her ear and sipped at a steaming mug of coffee.

"Ready?" Dad unfolded his newspaper.

"We're not still doing that are we?" Annalise asked, mock exasperation in her tone.

"Well, if you can't handle it anymore. American education ruining your mind and all that, then I suppose I'll have to represent the dark blue and handle the crossword myself." Dad drew a stub pencil from his pocket.

"Pencil?" Annalise snorted. "Amateur." She scooted her chair closer to his and they went to work.

This brought back memories. The two of them, both with their brows wrinkled in concentration, every Sunday morning. I'd hated it when I was younger, the way Dad somehow had a bond with Annalise that he never had with me. Now I realized it was a good thing. Their bond was strong, something different yet somehow the same as my bond with him.

"That's not even a word." Annalise laughed, the sound smoothing away the bad memories and leaving only butterflies darting around in my stomach.

Ellen came in carrying a plate of eggs, bacon, and pancakes. "Eat up. I might think twice about the pancakes, though."

"Oh, come on, Mom. I'm sure they're fine." Annalise paused the crossword and started serving out the food. When she took her first bite of pancake, she brought her napkin up and spit the bite right back out.

Laughter filled the dining room.

"Oh, shut up, all of you." Annalise smiled despite her words. The daggers from the previous night's dinner were gone. Instead, she was radiant, happy.

I may have given Howie a few bites of my pancake. He

didn't seem to mind the consistency.

We had a good breakfast, discussing the skiing and shopping we planned for the day. I intended to ski. The slopes were calling, the bitter wind from the previous day having died down overnight. The sun was out, making all the white gleam to a blinding shine.

"Well, I intend to hit Main Street." Ellen put the last of the plates in the sink. "Hard."

"Oh, dear." Dad kissed her on the top of her head. "I can already feel my pockets getting lighter."

"You coming, Anna?" Ellen asked.

"I think I'm ready to stretch my legs and do some skiing. It's been a while." She shimmied past where I stood in the doorframe. Her heat was there for a second and then gone, leaving me wanting. Her hair smelled like an intoxicating floral bouquet. It lingered in my nose, stealing any thoughts I'd had for a second.

"I think maybe I'll shop with you today." Dad said and draped his hands around her shoulders.

"You just want to keep me on a credit card leash."

Dad smiled. "Even so, my love."

I followed Annalise into the front hallway. She wrapped her scarf around her neck and donned her ski gear. I followed suit, insulating myself against the invigorating chill. The chalet was close to the gondola, so we went ahead and put on our ski boots.

I kept watching her move, the seductive lines of her body. I wished we were somewhere more private where I could be stripping her clothes off instead of the other way around. She avoided my gaze though I could see the color in her cheeks. It set me on fire.

Ellen and Dad bustled in behind us and threw on their jackets and scarves.

"Well, we're off. Be careful out on the slopes, kids." Ellen gave each of us a kiss on the cheek before taking Dad's arm and heading down the stairs. The door swung closed behind them, leaving Annalise and I alone.

I'd reached for the skis, my hand already resting on them. But when I lifted them, she looked up. Her gaze met mine and I saw the sudden blaze. I dropped the skis and took her in my arms before pressing a possessive kiss on her lips. She tried to back away, to escape me. *Not happening.* I squeezed her in my arms and forced her lips apart, pushing my tongue deeply into her mouth.

She beat at my sides, trying to escape my grasp. I pushed her away and turned her around before slamming her back into my chest and wrapping one hand around her throat. I worked my fingers under her turtleneck so it was skin on skin contact and tightened my grip. In one rough move, I shoved my hand down her pants and into her panties.

Just as I suspected, her panties were already soaked.

"Niles, please."

I tightened my hand until she was barely breathing and leaning against me as I swirled my fingers around her hot, wet clit. I slipped a finger inside her and her pussy clenched me in tighter. I didn't want it to be my finger. I needed it to be my cock that was already throbbing hard as a rock in my pants.

"Be a good girl for me," I whispered in her ear. "If you run, I'll catch you and punish you."

I stroked her clit harder. "Are you going to be good?"

She nodded. I released her throat and dropped to my knees so her ass was at eye level. I gripped her pants and panties and ripped them down her legs, revealing her beautiful plump ass. I yanked them all the way down past her knees. I needed my mouth buried in her sweet pussy lips, her juices running down my throat.

"Bend over."

She didn't move. I ran my hand up her leg, inner thigh, and then forced it into her wet heat. She squealed at the intrusion. I'd never felt anything more perfect.

"Over, Anna. Right now or you won't like what happens next." What happened next would be me balls deep in her pussy while I rough fucked her against the front door as she screamed.

Slowly, she obeyed.

"Good girl."

The further over she went, the more her pussy opened up to me. I removed my fingers from her and put a hand on either side of her ass. Her asshole was a little hidden flower right above her glistening pussy.

I couldn't control myself. I buried my face in her ass, and licked all of the wrinkled skin around her tight hole. I snaked my tongue down to her cunt to get a taste and licked her asshole as she moaned and shuddered. My cock strained against my pants, demanding to be inside where my tongue held sway.

She trembled, squeals turning to moans as my tongue pushed inside her wet heat. She gripped me, her body making promises my cock was desperate to take her up on. I slid my tongue even farther, to the hot bud desperate for attention. She jerked when I started flicking it, teasing it.

I gripped her thighs, not caring what sort of marks I was leaving. She was mine. I would mark her any way I wanted. I wanted to make her come like that, but my cock would not be denied any longer. After a few more licks I stood and grabbed her around the waist. I pushed her forward onto the stairs and ripped her pants and panties the rest of the way off. She was totally bare, her pussy swollen and ready. I couldn't have stopped if I'd tried.

I pulled her up by her hair and stripped her shirt off before gripping the back of her bra and yanking the material apart.

"Niles!"

I ignored her protest and shucked the bra off. Then I reached around and palmed both her tits as I fastened my teeth at her neck. She tasted sweet and slightly salty, her body covered with a fine sheen of sweat. I would cover her with more than that.

I kneaded her tits and then grabbed the hard nipples

between my thumb and forefinger. I twisted and pinched. She shuddered and moaned as I licked up her neck and made even more love bites along her fair skin. I switched to her other side, all the while still squeezing and pinching her. Once satisfied I'd marked her, I released her and pushed her down.

I unzipped my pants and pulled out my cock. She looked at me over her shoulder, her eyes a euphoric mix of desire and fear. She was perfectly situated one stair up, her pussy ready for my cock. I moved to her and pressed my head to her folds. She froze for a moment then took off. One stair, then another. I was on top of her in seconds. When I captured her, she cried out, the sound going straight to my cock.

"Niles, don't," she said, but her pussy was hot and wet. I knew she wanted it. I knew she wanted me to take it.

I gripped her hips hard. She needed to understand she was mine now. When we were together like this, I owned her. I raised a hand and brought it down on her ass with a loud crack. She squealed, and I was pleased to see my red handprint on her skin. I did it again, marking her other perfect ass cheek and she let out a strangled scream.

"I own you, Anna. All of you." I slapped her again, another cry from her lips.

"Say it." *Slap.*

"Say it, Anna. I won't stop until I hear it." *Slap.*

She turned to look back at me, tears in her eyes warring with the lust.

"You own me." Her breathy declaration was all I needed.

"Fuck right I do." I pushed my head inside her wet cunt, the constriction exquisite.

Her moan echoed up the stairs. All I could feel was her. All I could see, all I could think – her. I moved further inside, my legs straining with the need to fuck her raw. She rocked back into me, pushing me even deeper. *Bloody hell.* I reached up and took a handful of her hair, pulling her back into me as I started a steady rhythm.

She was so perfectly slick that I slid with no problem, my tip hitting her deepest part. Her breathing was fast. I was flat out panting, overwhelmed by the woman I had under my control and impaled on my cock. I gripped her hip and began slamming into her, yanking her onto my cock with each hard stroke.

We were in a direct line of sight from the front door. If Ellen or Dad came back for any reason, they'd get a front row view of us fucking. I didn't care. I wouldn't stop. Her body wouldn't let me. Our skin slapped and her moans grew louder. A tinkling sound mimicked our rhythm and I realized we were shaking the bells on the Christmas tree nearby. I should have thought it was funny, should have laughed. Instead, I pounded her harder, giving the bells a run for their money as her pussy tightened around me.

"You are such a hot little cunt, aren't you?" I gritted the words from between my teeth.

She responded by moving back harder against me and moaning low in her throat. I wanted to keep that sound to myself, to never let anyone else hear it. When she said I owned her, it wasn't just words. It was the truth. Emboldened by the thought, I pulled her up so her back was to my chest. I bit down on her shoulder as I kept my quick pace. I slid a hand down her stomach and stroked her hard nub, swollen and needy for my touch.

"Yes, please," she breathed.

I obliged, strumming her clit even as my balls drew up against me, desperate to shoot my load. Her muscles quivered and her pussy clamped down on me. I sucked her skin between my teeth.

"Don't come until I say, little slut."

"I can't stop. P-please, Niles."

"No. Not until I say. Not until my cock is spurting my cum deep in your pussy."

"Oh my god, Niles." Her voice was desperate and my name on her lips sent me over the edge too soon.

My cock surged inside her.

"Come. Now."

She came on a strangled scream, her pussy milking me as I pumped in jerky thrusts, the pleasure short-circuiting any smooth movements. I plunged into her until every last drop was gone. She fell forward and caught herself with her hands. She gave me a look over her shoulder, her eyes glazed with the same euphoria I felt in my bones.

I had bitten into her shoulder harder than I'd intended, leaving a half moon along the top and back. Instead of regret, I felt pride. She was mine. She should bear my marks, just like the ones on her ass from my palms.

She scooted up the stairs, and I winced when my cock slid from its favorite spot. I gripped her hips and ripped her back to me. I crushed her in my arms and kissing her neck, gently this time.

"Did I hurt you?" I whispered in her ear.

"No, I just. I need to—"

"I need you to know I'll never hurt you again, Anna." I meant every word.

She sighed as I kissed up her earlobe and smoothed my hands around her waist. "I want to believe you. I do. But this ... this thing we're doing. Whatever it is. It doesn't change the past."

"I can't change it. It's true. But I can make it up to you. I keep trying. What else can I do?"

She relaxed against me the slightest bit. "You're definitely making a grade-A effort. I'll give you that." The smile in her voice soothed my frantic heartbeat.

"Good. I'll keep making it as long as you let me."

"No promises, Niles."

"Right." I smiled, my heart warming at the sliver of a chance she was giving me. "No promises."

CHAPTER FIVE
ANNALISE

I STARED HARD AT my reflection. I'd cleaned up and gotten dressed—again—after the incident on the stairs. Niles was waiting for me, but I was trying to figure out who was staring back at me from the mirror.

I had just let Niles fuck me not once, but twice. I shook my head, doing my best to ignore the patches of pink high on my cheeks, the slightest hint of exhilaration still flowing through my heart. *What am I doing?*

Fucking your stepbrother over Christmas break was taking the "good will toward men" part of the season too far. I groaned when I thought about what Mom and Brent would think if they found out. Mortification spread throughout my body, tamping down the rushing endorphins of only moments before. I needed to stop this, to put an end to what was going on between Niles and me.

"Anna?" Niles' voice floated up the stairs and into my room.

"Coming!" I yelled back and then realized what I'd said. *Palm meet forehead.*

Thankfully he didn't say anything as I hurried down the stairs and past him. He did smile, though. I had never realized what a gorgeous smile he had, how the dimples appeared and made him even more boyishly handsome. *Stop, Anna.*

I donned my scarf, hat, and gloves. Niles was ready to go, holding our skis and poles. I hadn't intended to ski all day with him. But I wouldn't get too far without my skis.

He leaned the equipment against his chest and pulled the door open for me, mischief still in his baby blues. "After you, as always."

I strode out and down the steps. He followed behind and we crossed the street toward the gondola entrance. He put his hand at my lower back, guiding me around the other skiers and past the icy patches. I didn't need his help, but something about the slight pressure at my lower back comforted me. The ache inside reminded me of what we'd just done, but somehow his steady hand spoke more about our newfound truce. Well, if rough sex under our parents' noses could be called a "truce."

We got in line to ride up, families crowding inside, waiting for the next gondola. He was at my back, his warm breath playing at my ear. It was as if all my nerve endings belonged to him or were somehow attuned only to him. I strained to hear any change in his breathing to sense any shift in his body.

"Ready?" he asked.

"Yeah." We stepped into the gondola. He took the seat right next to me and threw his arm around my shoulders. It was easy, right.

Two giggling girls took the seats opposite us. They both stopped chattering for a moment and gawked at Niles. I glanced over at him. He wasn't looking at the blondes. His gaze was glued to me. He gave an easy smile and squeezed my shoulder.

We began our trip up the mountain. The snow was thick and white beneath us, only ski lines marring the smooth surface. Niles kept his arm around me, keeping me grounded even as we floated up and away to the middle of the mountain. The two girls chattered — talking about their plans for the rest of the day or what they wanted for Christmas.

The sounds faded to the background and all I could sense was him right next to me. The man who'd made me come harder than I ever had in my life. I shook my head, as if that would clear it.

"It's okay, Anna. Don't overthink it." His low voice was steady and soothing and his pressure increased on my shoulder, warmth transferring from him to me.

How could he know the storm roiling inside me? And worse, how could he know to say exactly what I needed to hear?

"Are you, um, are you single?" one of the blondes blurted. It appeared she'd surreptitiously unzipped the top of her ski jacket during our ride so that her cleavage was proudly displayed.

Niles pulled me into his side. "Do I look single?"

Blondie frowned and zipped up her jacket. Her cohort snickered until Blondie elbowed her in the ribs.

We rode the rest of the way in silence, though my smile may have spoken louder than words.

Once we came to a stop, the blondes exited in a huff. Niles led me out and we sat to get our skis situated. He was attentive, helping me snap everything in place before starting on his own skis. I stared down at his thick red hair, made markedly brighter by the backdrop of white. When he looked up at me with his sapphire eyes, a host of butterflies sprang up in my stomach.

"All set?" He stepped into his skis.

"Yes."

"Which run are you feeling?"

"Oh, we don't have to, I mean, you don't have to go on the slopes with me. I stick to the medium runs, blues mostly. You're probably more of a double black diamond guy or something." I wanted him to stay with me, but I didn't want to ruin his day with the bunny hills.

"Blues are fine by me. If you remember, dark blues are my thing." He winked, devilish and handsome.

"Are we back to the rowing again?" I laughed. "Blue versus blue?"

"Indeed we are. I'm glad things can always come back around to what's most important in life." He stood and readied his poles. "After you, my lady."

I took off, gliding up the slope until we reached the open ski lift. After a short wait, we hopped on and sailed up the mountain a bit further. The sun was high and bright, the snow beneath us blinding.

"Perfect day to ski." He put his hand on my knee and massaged it, his long fingers splayed against the white of my pants.

"I know. Brent and Mom should have saved shopping for later." I didn't know what I'd actually said. I could only think about his hand on my knee, his fingers, the way they'd been inside me not that much earlier.

"What slope are you thinking?"

"Pussyfoot," I answered, once again, without thinking.

He laughed and moved his hand further up my thigh just a bit. Thank god I had clamped my oversized Jackie-O sunglasses on or he would have seen the intense red blush that crept into my cheeks.

"That's one of my favorites, as well."

I know.

Reality was muffled, the only sound the wind and the only sensation his hand on my leg, rubbing circles against my inner thigh. I slid from the lift and onto the platform, and he followed. We skied to the top of the run.

Before I could start down, he tightened up the scarf around my neck. Then he pulled a tube of lip protectant from his pocket and smoothed it along my lips. Strangely erotic, he looked into my eyes as he did it. I should have felt ridiculous – a grown woman getting babied like that – but I felt protected, happy even.

Once he was done with my lips, he quickly smoothed

36

some on his own and stowed it back into his pocket.

"Ready?" he smiled and my breath caught.

"Yes." He was melting me bit by bit, just a snowman on a hot day.

I broke my gaze and looked down the slope. The snow was perfect, still smooth from a recent grooming.

I pushed my poles into the powder and stroked lightly down the slope. Niles was at my elbow in a moment, both of us gliding easily down the curving trail of white. The wind hummed through the trees along the edges and chilled the few spots of exposed skin on my face. I didn't care. The feeling of easy speed was exhilarating. There were only a few other skiers around us, leaving us in our own little bubble.

"Never knew simply sliding down a hill could be so much fun, yeah?" he said over the sound of our skis.

"I've never really thought about it like that, but I guess that's what we're doing." I laughed.

He returned my smile before digging in his poles and shooting out ahead. He looked back and waggled his eyebrows. A challenge. He may have been a double black diamond skier, but he wasn't going to beat me on my favorite run.

I dug my poles in and shot down after him. He turned back forward and got serious, pushing himself farther out in front. I tucked in, and flew down, right on his tail. He glanced over his shoulder, a look of surprise on his face at how close I'd already gotten. Then he dug in harder and faster, both of us flying past other skiers as Niles called out "on the left" or "on the right" as we went.

I had always been competitive. In school, in soccer, in anything that I felt I excelled at. I didn't excel at skiing, but I would be damned if I would let Niles beat me.

I pumped my arms, digging the poles in even as they skittered along the surface. We were racing down the mountain, the scenery blurring in a green and white wave of speed. My heart was pumping and my knees started to burn from the tension. I bent them further and leaned into it, barreling ahead and getting to Niles' elbow.

He glanced to me, a smile plastered in his face. There was a matching one on mine as we stopped pushing and simply let the hill take us. We glided over the snow, the whisper and whir of our skis the only competing sound with the wind.

We reached the part where the hill turned slightly to the right and joined the main run. He looked over at me, now neck and neck. He didn't see the skier in red who'd eased into the run only a few feet ahead of him. I screamed, but it was too late. The impact sent the red skier onto his back and Niles went flying.

CHAPTER SIX
NILES

I DIDN'T PASS OUT. I wished I had, but I didn't. I slid down the snow on my back before friction finally made an appearance and slowed me down. My sunglasses were long gone and the sun was blinding me. Pain radiated from my left leg, along with less intense aches from other parts of my body.

"Niles!" Anna's voice, or rather a scream.

I was still sliding, lazily now. Then I bumped into something. It blocked the sun. Big and blue, it was talking to me.

"—quite a spill. You okay? Ski patrol will be here in a minute."

Anna appeared above me and she dropped to her knees at my side. She pushed her sunglasses on top of her head and showed me her beautiful eyes. I smiled, but I think it came across as more of a wince.

"Oh my god, Niles. Are you okay? What hurts?"

"How's the other guy?" I tried to sit up, but couldn't quite make it.

Anna pressed a hand to my shoulder. "Lie still. I'm going to check you. What hurts the worst?" She was so close, the concern in her eyes lighting me up from the inside.

"The other guy?"

"He's fine, Niles." She blew a strand of hair out of her face in one sexy, exasperated move. "Just had the wind knocked out of him. Now, where?"

She peered into my eyes, one after the other.

"Left calf."

She disappeared from my view and I cursed. Pressure at my knee and then lower, her small hands working deftly. The pain grew the further she went until I groaned.

"It's broken." She came back in my field of vision. I smiled.

"That's not a good thing, Niles." She frowned.

"I know. I just—"

"I see ski patrol further up the run. They'll be here in a minute." The big blue bear of a man was still standing off to the side, watching and directing traffic.

"Where else hurts?" She ran her hands along my chest and down to my abs. "Any of this bother you?"

"No, but keep going with the massage."

She rolled her eyes but still gave me a small smile before feeling down my arms. I was achy, but nothing held a candle to the pain in my leg. The cold of the snow seeped into my back and I wanted to sit up, but I didn't try it lest I make my nurse angry.

"There's another spot, too."

She paused and looked at me expectantly.

"Just south of my navel and north of my upper thighs."

The big blue bear laughed. Anna smacked me on the arm and then held her hand to her mouth with horror.

She looked like a snow angel. "It's okay, Anna. I had that hit coming."

"He did," agreed blue bear.

The purr of an engine approached, and it wasn't long before I was loaded up and carted down the mountain. Anna rode along with me, worry painting her face and coloring her dark eyes.

At the ER and then before surgery, she held my hand and kept a watch. It was as if she'd already gone into doctor mode.

She was even waiting when I woke up from surgery, along with Dad and a worried Ellen.

Ellen hugged my neck with the strength of ten blue bears. When my eyes started to bulge, Dad pulled her away and I lay back against the stack of pillows in the hospital bed. Anna held my other hand.

"Well at least you're getting along with your sister." Dad smiled.

Anna cringed and let my hand go. I wanted to grab it back.

"I meant it as a compliment, Annalise."

"Who cares?" Ellen asked. "I'm just glad we're all in one piece. Well, we all are now thanks to the rod in your leg."

Anna backed away from the bed and sat. She looked drained.

I glanced at the windows behind her. It was dark outside.

"What time is it?" The haze from the meds was still clouding things for me.

"A little after ten." Dad patted me on the arm. "Glad you're all right, son."

"Thanks." I couldn't take my eyes off Anna. I wanted her to rest, to stop worrying, to give me her smile again.

"That late already?" Ellen asked and then swore under her breath. "Oh no, Howie hasn't been out in ages!"

"You stay here. I'll go and let him out." Dad picked up his coat from the sofa near the door.

"No." I shook my head. "Everyone go home and get some sleep. I'll be fine."

Ellen put her hands on her hips, a classic stonewall move of hers. "Someone should stay, Niles, what if—"

"I'll stay." Anna leaned back in her chair, apparently

unwilling to budge.

"Are you sure?" Ellen glanced from me to Anna, trepidation in her eyes.

"It's fine Mom, really. I need to get used to all this if I'm going to go to med school, right?"

"Well ..."

Dad looked from me to Anna and smiled the slightest bit. "I think they'll be all right. Come on, let's go. We'll have the house to ourselves. Maybe we can get up to some funny business."

Ellen blushed. "Brent! At a time like this when your son is—hang on—what are you..."

Ellen kept scolding even as she allowed dad to help her with her coat and led her to the door.

"See you in the morning." Dad gave a knowing look from Anna and back to me again before escorting a tittering Ellen from the room.

"That still grosses me out." Anna propped her head on her hand.

"What, our parents getting it on?"

Anna groaned. "Yes, that." She rubbed her eyes with the heels of her palms.

"Come on." I shifted over, ignoring the pain radiating from the cast on my leg. It was a dull ache, whatever pain medicine they'd given me doing its job.

She shook her head. "I'll just sleep on the couch over there." But then she met my eyes, and I could see she was tempted.

I scooted further and groaned. She was up in an instant, leaning over me. "What, what happened? Do you need more pillows?"

My plan worked. She was close enough so I could grab her and drag her over the rail. She squeaked with surprise as I settled her into the bed next to me.

"Gotcha." I lay back, somehow drained from that small exertion.

"I can't sleep in your bed—"

"You can and you will." I inhaled her scent – some sort of fruity lotion and her shampoo. "I need to be attended to and you're just the pre-med student to do it."

She tried to sit up and away from me, but I clamped my hand on her like a vise.

She sighed. "Fine. I'll stay, Niles. I'll stay. Just let me take my jacket off. And my shoes."

"That's more like it." I relaxed and watched her strip off her outer layer. Her breasts were perfectly round against her fleecy top, begging to be touched. "Get under the covers."

"No." She stripped her shoes off and tossed them next to the bed.

I gripped the sheet and ripped it from under her like a magician with a tablecloth. "Yes. Get under here with me."

"What if the nurse comes i—"

The door swung open, and a nurse came in, right on cue. Dark skin and eyes, she had a friendly smile and a clipboard. She grinned when she saw Anna and me snuggling in the bed. Anna stiffened and moved away. *Not a chance.* I pulled her into my side.

"Nothing better than a little company when you're trying to recover." The nurse shuffled up to me and checked the machine hooked up to my IV. "You're still getting pain meds – the good stuff – for the next couple of hours. Enjoy it while you can." She fiddled with some buttons and the machine beeped.

"All right. You're all set. You two need anything, just hit the call button and I'll be in here in two shakes. Try and get some rest." She marked a few things off her clipboard. Then she winked at me and squeaked her rubber soles away from us before hitting the lights and pulling the door closed.

"Alone at last." I relaxed and hit the button to lay the bed all the way back. "Get comfy, Anna. I want you here when I wake up. If you're not, this cast won't stop me from punishing you and enjoying every second of it."

43

A sound caught in her throat at the threat and my cock twitched. But the swirl of morphine or whatever it was coursed through my blood made my eyes close. She settled in next to me, snuggling into my side but careful not to touch my cast. I pulled her tighter, forcing her to put her head on my chest. The tendrils of her hair tickled my nose as I drifted off to sleep.

***

The nurse was back. "Didn't mean to wake you sugar," she whispered.

Anna slept soundly on my chest. I blinked hard a few times and the dull ache in my leg went up a few notches.

I must have grimaced because the nurse said, "We've cut out the hard stuff, but I just pushed something different in your IV. Not as strong, but it should kick in shortly."

"What time is it?" I asked.

"About three a.m. or so. I'll be back around in a couple hours. Get on back to sleep." She glanced down to Anna. "She looks like a perfect angel, you know that?"

"She is."

The nurse smiled, warm and wise. "That's the right answer, young man." Then she left, once again closing the door.

Anna shifted on my chest and moved her head to rest into the crook of my neck. Her tits pressed into my side and her knee was slung over my thigh. Her breaths against my skin were like a spark. The spark turned into embers, and when she made a soft sigh in her sleep, I was alight.

The pain in my leg was nothing compared to my demanding shaft. It tented my hospital gown and the sheet on top of it.

"Anna," I whispered and kissed the crown of her head. I smoothed my hand up and down her back and she moved against me, pressing her tits even harder into my side.

Her hand smoothed across my chest. I grabbed it and

moved it down to my cock. I wrapped her fingers around my shaft and groaned at the feeling. She let out a gasp and woke.

She looked up at me. "What are you—"

I claimed her mouth and kept my hand on top of hers, moving her fingers up and down, from base to tip. Each stroke had my hips straining upward. I didn't feel my leg. All I felt was the pleasure in her grip. I licked along her lips and sank my tongue inside. She moaned and began stroking me herself. I let go and reached to her hair, grabbing a handful and crushing her to me as her hand worked my cock.

She couldn't get her hand all the way closed around my length, but she was trying, increasing the delicious pressure moment by moment. I could have come just from her hand, but I wanted more. I wanted her on top of me, her slick cunt milking me.

I broke our kiss. "Strip."

She glanced to the door. "But the nurse—"

"Won't be back for hours." I pushed her until she was sitting and started yanking the hem of her shirt up.

"But the door doesn't lock!" she hissed and tried to slap my hand away.

I grabbed a fistful of her hair close to her scalp. "My leg's broken, but I'll still master you, Anna. I know your panties get wet when I say that. I want them to. It's true. So you can either fight me and lose anyway or cooperate. I would generally prefer your fight, but the leg makes it a bit more difficult."

She glanced down to the cast hidden beneath the sheet and propped up on pillows.

"You are going to be naked, your tits bouncing as you ride my cock, one way or another." I yanked her shirt up again.

She sighed, seemingly resigned to her fate. I would have fought her and spanked her plump ass, but this way was easier given the circumstances. We'd have plenty of time for discipline once I'd healed up.

She peeled her shirt off and unhooked her bra. She glanced to the door every so often. That would stop as soon as she slid down on my cock. Her smell surrounded me and I wanted to taste between her legs.

She got to her knees and unbuttoned her pants, pushing them and her panties down before working them off. I fisted my cock as she undressed, as bit by bit of her gorgeous body came into my greedy view.

I ran my hand up and down my length, pretending it was her small hand again. I pushed the sheet down and her gaze locked on my slick head. When her tongue darted to her lips, I couldn't take another second without her being impaled on me.

"Straddle me."

She hesitated. I put my free hand around her pretty neck. "Do it, Anna."

She swallowed and opened her mouth to protest. I squeezed. She didn't say a word. She slowly straddled me, taking care not to touch my cast. At that point, I didn't give a shit if she kicked the damn thing as long as I was balls deep in her cunt within the next five seconds.

I released her neck and hit the button on the bed to put me in more of a sitting position. Her tits needed to be in my mouth as she rode me. I flicked on the light behind us, a soft glow in the dark room, then I yanked off my hospital shift, the snap buttons popping loose easily, and dropped it to the floor.

Tucking my thumb beneath my cock, I positioned it straight up. She eased onto it. I didn't want slow, I wanted it all. Right then. I let go of the button on the bed and gripped her shoulder, pushing her down until every inch of me was embedded inside her slick pussy. She bit her lip and moaned, but I couldn't stop. I licked up her collar bone as she adjusted, her cunt squeezing me in the most pleasant vise.

I gripped her hips and lifted her before sliding her back

down to earth. "That's it." My fingers would bruise her. I didn't care. Her body was mine.

Her tits rubbed against my chest, the nipples demanding attention, and I would bloody well give it. I nuzzled down her chest until I came to the soft flesh. I bit into her breast lightly, leaving teeth marks on the ripe tip. She moaned and kept the pace I'd set for her, working my cock in and out.

I nipped at her dusky nipple, teasing it lightly. Her hips momentarily lost their rhythm and she moaned, but my hands guided her back to it. I lifted and dropped, lifted and dropped, her ass slapping against my thighs. She hadn't looked at the door once since I took up residence inside her, where I belonged.

Her dark eyes were focused on me. Her breaths were shallowing and she squealed when I bit down on her budded peak. I didn't let up, rolling it back and forth between my teeth as she bounced on my cock.

Her moans grew louder and she threw her head back. I thrust up into her harder and harder as she plummeted onto my shaft. I released her nipple and sucked her breast into my mouth. I latched onto her perfect tit and lashed her with my tongue as my balls drew up, ready to shoot my load inside her. I refused, not until she was crying my name. I wanted her gone, checked out of her headspace and awash in nothing but the feeling of me inside her, beneath her, all over her.

"Such a hot slut, riding this cock."

Her eyes lit when I talked dirty, upping the fire even higher.

She ran her hands through my hair and gripped, the sting of sensation spurring my hips faster, harder. I wanted to punish her, needed her to know I was the one in control even as she rode me. I moved my hand to her clit and rubbed the swollen numb with my thumb.

She moaned, the sound echoing around the room and likely audible in the hallway. I loved every single second of it.

"You going to come for me, Anna?"

"Yes." It was a breath prayer more than an answer.

"Come all over my cock like a good girl?"

"Yes, please." Her voice was sex. My shaft pulsed, desperate to coat her cunt with my seed.

"Say my name, Anna. Say it when you come. I want to hear who's making you feel so good." I pressed harder against her clit and rubbed up and down to her quickening rhythm.

"It's you. You. I need to come. I'm there. Please."

God, I loved it when she begged. I intended to make her beg so many more times. Enough to fill every nook and cranny of my mind with her words, her whimpers.

I surged up, getting every last bit of contact as her tight cunt throttled my cock.

"Say it and you can come, Anna. Who's making you come?"

"Nile—" The word turned into a strangled cry as she rocketed down onto my cock and let go. Her pussy crushed me as she repeated my name, her body shuddering with each wave of pleasure. I couldn't take the pressure, the sounds, the feeling of her body against mine as she gave herself to me.

I gripped her hips and held her down on my cock. I groaned as the first spurt erupted into her and bit her shoulder as the tsunami of release washed over me. I shoved up, lashing her with my cum as her pussy took every last bit I had to offer. When I couldn't give anything else, I pulled her to my chest and lay back. I hit the button so that we were lying flat again. She was still panting though her breaths were slowing. I whipped the sheet back over her, though I hated losing sight of her luscious skin, and I clicked off the light.

We simply lay for a while, breathing and coming down from the high. My leg reminded me of its existence, blood rushing to it instead of my dick. It was still inside her, barely.

"This is a mistake." Her voice was so soft now.

"No, it's not, love."

"It is. Our parents are married." She ran her fingertips down my chest and rested her head over my heart. "They would freak."

"Nah. They'd be glad that we aren't at each others' throats all the time."

"We weren't always fighting, I guess." Her eyelashes whispered against my skin, a pleasant sensation.

"I was always being a todger. I knew it then. I know it now. Only difference is now I regret it." I rubbed my hands along her back.

"Well, you were. That's true." I could feel her nibbling at her lower lip. "But maybe I should have cut you more slack. You were having a hard time with a whole new life in Dallas, whole new family, all of that. I guess I wasn't exactly welcoming."

I remembered clearly the skeptical look on her face when my father and I pulled up in front of her house. The day we'd first met – just a casual get-together while our parents were dating. I hadn't been looking forward to meeting Annalise or her mother. Annalise had watched me like I was some sort of invading insect. I also hadn't expected such a chilly welcome. Then again, I was so angry about everything – my mother, my father, moving to the States. But now, with her in my arms, everything was different.

"We started on the wrong foot." I dropped kisses in her hair.

"We did."

"I'd like to start over. I kind of hope we already have."

She nibbled at her lip a bit more and then let out a sigh. "We have. Clean slate. Erase the past."

"Hang on a tick." I smoothed a hand down to her ass. You aren't erasing the past two days, are you?"

She giggled and something inside my heart melted.

"No. I'll keep these in the positive column."

I gave her ass a squeeze and wished it bore some of my handprints. Next time.

"I should get dressed." She tried to roll away. My dick slid out and I groaned, but I wasn't letting her go so easily.

"No, wait a while. Just relax. You're under the covers. Nurse won't know."

She yawned. "I guess you're right."

She nuzzled against me and after a short while, her breaths became relaxed and even. I loved every moment of it – the sex, of course – but the feeling of her in my arms even more so.

CHAPTER SEVEN
ANNALISE

A SHARP INTAKE OF breath woke me. I sat up.

Mom and Brent were in the doorway. *Shit.* I had fallen asleep in Niles' bed, naked.

Mom reached up and slapped her hand across Brent's eyes. I looked down and scrambled to pull up the sheet. My tits had just been hanging out for all to see – but mostly Brent – because I'd been so startled.

"What in the name of all that is holy are you *doing*, Anna!" Mom's voice was probably heard on other floors of the hospital.

My neurons couldn't fire. I couldn't even begin to come up with a plausible explanation for why I was naked in my stepbrother's bed. "I just, we're just—"

"We're together." Niles sat up and drew the sheet tighter around me.

Brent slapped mom's hand away and took in the full scene, *sans* breasts this time.

"You *can't* be together. Your siblings for Christ's sake!" An edge of hysteria crept into Mom's voice. Usually I would tell her she was overreacting, but at this point, after what I'd done, maybe she was right to lose it a bit.

"Oh, sure they can." Brent shrugged and strode the rest of the way in before plopping down on the sofa. He beamed at us, clearly not an awkward bone in his body.

"But they're siblings, Brent." Mom zombie walked, unable to take her eyes from us, and collapsed on the couch next to Brent.

Niles stroked my back before apparently thinking better of it and giving me a reassuring squeeze.

"They aren't blood, Ellen. This sort of thing is common in England. Step siblings getting married and such. It's only a *thing* to you yanks. It's not a big deal. Truly, love."

"Whoa, we aren't getting married or anything. I mean, not that I don't like him, but it's not ... I mean, we aren't ... all we've done is—" (*fuck*).

"Started a relationship." Niles jumped in before I could ruin it further. I looked back at him and he smiled, far more confidently and sexily than any man should be allowed. "It's brand new to us, too."

"I just don't know what to think." Mom leaned back against the sofa and stared at the drop ceiling. "I mean, I would never have guessed this. Brent, did you guess this or something." She whipped her head to him. "Did you *know?*"

"Of course not, love. I just thought they were acting the polar opposite of how they used to around each other. I hoped for the best and—" he gestured to Niles and me "—the best happened."

I began to feel more and more creeped out as Mom appeared shell-shocked and Brent looked happy as a lark. I was still naked and I was almost certain I could make out Niles' morning wood beneath the sheet.

I cleared my throat. "Well, I really need to get dressed, so if you two could give me a second."

Mom stood and gave me another bewildered look before walking to the door. Brent rose and followed her. He turned back to us and mouthed "*she'll be fine*," before leading her from the room and closing the door.

I pulled my knees up and dropped my head onto them. "'Fucked up' isn't a strong enough phrase to describe that."

He rubbed my back some more. It was comforting, but I wasn't sure if I wanted to be comforted right then. I slid away from him and pulled on my clothes.

"Don't do that." He sighed.

"Do what?"

"Get all up in your head and regret us, yeah?"

I yanked my turtleneck down and turned to him. "There is no *us*, Niles."

Hurt flashed across his blue eyes, but somehow, I felt the pain, too. It was as if I had jammed a splinter into my heart. But it was true. We weren't a couple. We were practically strangers. I'd let my body make my decisions and it had to stop. Even if he'd changed, it didn't matter. Mom was right.

"I need to go back to the house. Get cleaned up." I didn't look him in the eye. I couldn't.

He sighed. "Fine, Annalise. It's fine." Resignation and disappointment all rolled into four words.

Tears rose in my eyes. I rushed to the door and almost collided with the nurse. I sprinted past her, past Mom and Brent in the hall, and burst into the stairwell right as my tears started falling. *What was I doing?* I took the stairs as fast as I could, even as my vision blurred.

***

I stayed in my room, only coming down to the kitchen for food when I knew Mom and Brent were out. Mom came by and knocked a couple of times – the second time saying she was sorry for acting like she did at the hospital. I gave in and told her it was fine, but I didn't open the door. I knew my eyes were puffy and I looked a wreck. Funny, I hadn't shed any tears over my last ex-boyfriend, Gavin. Now I was a blubbering mess after Niles.

He came home from the hospital the next day. I heard

53

Mom and Brent helping him into the house. They set him up in the living room on the couch near the enormous tree. I imagined him sitting there, all wrapped up in a cast like a sad Christmas present. It would have been funny if he were the old Niles and I was the old Annalise, but we weren't.

I felt ridiculous for running at the hospital, for the way I'd reacted, for the things I'd said. I wanted to apologize, but I was too embarrassed. Instead, I maintained my hideout and watched as the snow fell out my window.

I tried to do schoolwork on my laptop, but my thoughts kept straying down the stairs. Niles was like an itch I couldn't scratch. The notes and reading I needed to do quickly fell by the wayside once I realized I'd read the same sentence about ten times over and still didn't know what it said.

I goofed around on the Internet, reading about the blues of Oxford and Cambridge, the town where Niles had grown up, and his courses of study. I even found a picture of him with his shirtless rowing team. They all had their arms hung around each others' shoulders and smiled into the camera. Niles was in the center. I could see it now, how he could be the heart of a team.

I stared at his easy smile (and, yes, his hard body) for a ridiculous amount of time. I leaned back in my bed, heat racing through me as I thought about him, the things he'd done, the way he'd treated me – just the way I wanted and needed.

My stomach growled and I realized I hadn't eaten since breakfast. It was after ten. Mom and Brent had already gone to their room. Niles had to be doped up and asleep. Still, I didn't want to risk running into him. My stomach growled again, this time more of a roar, and made the decision for me.

I crept to my door. Silence. I opened it slowly, trying to ward off any creaking hinges. It worked. No noise. I padded down the hallway and peeked over the balustrade.

The living room below was dark, but the twinkle of the Christmas tree illuminated enough for me to see Niles asleep on the sofa.

I prayed my stomach would be quiet and tiptoed down the stairs. I glanced over to Niles every so often. He looked beautiful, his face serene in sleep. One arm was slung over his head and his t-shirt had risen up his stomach, revealing his abs. An ache went through me that was related to an entirely different sort of hunger, but I pushed it away.

I eased through the hallway and into the kitchen. I let out the breath I'd been holding and opened the fridge. Everything looked good at this point, even the bottle of mustard. I grabbed up some lunch meat and got the bread from the pantry. I was doing well with the ninja routine. I made a sandwich and eyed a bag of potato chips desperately, but I left them alone. Too much noise.

I returned to the island to grab my sandwich, but I was shoved forward and a hand clapped over my mouth, covering my scream.

A hard body behind me and warm breath at my ear. "Thought it would be that easy?"

Niles pushed his hard cock against my ass and my panties drenched. His other hand ripped my pajama bottoms down. His cock was already free, pressing into my ass.

"Not a fucking sound, Anna." He released my mouth and splayed his fingers on my back, pushing me down onto the island. "You brought this on yourself."

His head nudged to my entrance and I couldn't stop the soft moan that lofted from me.

"Tell me you deserve this, Anna. You deserve worse – but I can't spank you like you need, not until later. This will have to do for now. But I want to hear you ask for it. Tell me."

I was panting as he rubbed his stiff head all over my pussy lips. He pushed me down harder, my breasts pressing against the granite.

"I-I deserve it."

"Too right you do." He shoved inside me and I jerked forward, but there was nowhere to go. The thin sliver of pain turned into the finest pleasure as he withdrew and sank inside me again.

I moaned again, incapable of keeping the sensations inside. His fingers clenched my back at the sound and he began pistoning into me, wet sounds echoing around the room. I only hoped they didn't make it up the stairs to our parents' room.

I was black powder and his cock was the match. My pussy tensed with each strong stroke. I felt his punishment, his aggression as he worked it out on me. I wanted every bit of it, every emotion he could give. Pouring it into me, he fucked me perfectly. My face against the cold granite and his cock inside my hot pussy. He grunted with the effort of his hard strokes, deep and masculine sounds that spoke to me on a primal level. I couldn't move, my legs trapped against the cabinets and my torso prone on the island. I was his to use.

His cock thickened inside me as he thrusted. He snaked a hand to my clit and rubbed in vicious swirling strokes.

"You don't deserve this, Anna." His voice was guttural, animal. "I shouldn't let you come. I shouldn't, but I want you so fucking sated you'll never think of running again." He hammered me harder the more he spoke, his fingers working the pleasure from deep within me to the surface. "You going to run again?" He took his fingers away, the buildup ebbing. *No!*

"No!"

"You sure?" He flicked his fingers across my clit.

"I'm sure. Never. Please, Niles."

He stroked me full on again, making me writhe beneath him even as he kept me immobile on the stone.

"Then come, Anna. All over my cock."

He surged forward harder, his thighs slapping my ass as

I rose all the way onto my tiptoes. A few more pushes and I was gone, shooting skyward and exploding. I bit down on my hand to keep my moans quiet. I didn't know if I'd succeeded, my shuddering pussy taking precedence over anything else. It was a hard come, the tension seizing Niles' cock and dragging it further inside as I trembled at the explosion rocking me from head to toe.

"Bloody hell," he gritted out before pulling his cock free and grunting. I felt the hot spurts coating my pussy and ass. He shot all over me even as my pussy kept clamping down, wanting his length back inside.

When he was done, he reached next to me and grabbed a kitchen towel. He wiped me clean and then collapsed on my back, still breathing hard.

"You're mine, Anna. All of you. If you run, I'll catch you. There is no one else for you. Only me. Is that clear?"

He asked so much. But something clicked inside me, something that had never ever been set in motion before. "Yes."

"I mean it, Anna."

I took a deep breath and let it out. "I do, too. I'm yours."

EPILOGUE
ANNALISE

Christmas, One Year Later

"BEAT THEM AGAIN. AND you rowing for your life. Tell it again!" Brent clapped his knee and laughed.

We all sat on the sofa near the even gaudier Christmas tree Mom had decorated this year. Niles' arm was around my shoulders and I snuggled into his side. I hadn't seen him since fall break. Skyping and phone sex were great, but just being near him was making me hot all over, and in one spot in particular. His scent, clean and delicious, was all I could smell. His voice all I could hear.

He rubbed my arm, up and down his hand moved in a smooth, easy, nonstop motion. He was playing it cool for our parents, but I could sense the heat beneath the surface. I couldn't wait for it to explode outward in a flare of energy.

He obliged Brent and started his story of rowing victory again. "Well, the Cambridge cunts—"

"Niles!" Mom clutched at where her pearl strand should have been.

"Oh, it's an accurate description, love." Brent kissed Mom on her neck, lingering a bit too long.

"Get a room, you two." Niles laughed. It probably sounded normal to them. To me, it was strained. He rubbed my arm faster, as if anticipation was infecting his movements.

"Well, it is late, love. How about we go on upstairs and discuss the word 'cunt' a bit more, yeah?"

Mom slapped Brent's hand off her knee, but she stood. "I'm taking him upstairs before he embarrasses himself anymore. Goodnight, you two."

Brent rose, as well, and followed Mom to the stairs. He copped a feel on her ass as they went and I looked away, mortified. "I'd venture to say what I'm about to do to you will make my family proud, not embarrassed, love."

"I see where you get it from," I whispered and nuzzled Niles.

Niles smiled down at me, more predatory than amused. As soon as our parents' door clicked closed, he was on top of me. His lips on my neck, his hands yanking my top down so he could get to my breasts. They were braless, just as he'd instructed. I wore a skirt, far too short for the season, also as he'd instructed. But I'd broken his last rule... on purpose. I'd worn panties.

His mouth was hot on my neck, his teeth demanding my attention even as he twined one hand in my hair and thumbed my nipple with the other.

"I have wanted to fuck you raw for the past two hours. Since I first stepped foot in here and saw you dressed like that. Perfect little tart. All mine. Just like I told you. Did you know that?"

"I may have had an idea." I smiled.

He squeezed my breast so hard it almost hurt and then let off. I sighed as he kissed to my mouth and claimed it as his own. His kiss was rough, devouring me just as surely as a wolf.

He yanked my legs up onto the couch so I was fully on my back, and spread them apart. His cock was hard against me, promising me so much. I dug my nails through his shirt and into his back before yanking up on the fabric. He sat back and ripped it over his head, showing me his sun kissed chest and sculpted abs.

"Niles." It was all I could say, all I could think.

He reached down to his pants and unzipped before pulling out his cock. He hissed and gave it a smooth stroke before turning his eyes to my skirt. I thrilled at what he'd do when he saw I broke the rules.

He ran his hand up my thigh slowly, pushing the skirt higher and higher until his eyes fastened on the lace between my legs. His nostrils flared and he dug his fingers into my thigh.

"You've been bad, Anna." He put his palm over my pussy and rubbed me, the heel of his hand working my clit beneath the fabric.

I moved my hips up to him. "Yes."

He smiled, cruel and beautiful. "I hope you didn't like these, love."

He clutched my panties and ripped them off in one easy move. Then he put the head of his cock to my pussy and smoothed it down my clit to my entrance.

I wanted all of it, every last bit. I'd craved it, dreamed about it, woke up drenched with sweat and masturbating to it.

"Say it, Anna. Say it and I'll give you everything you need. But I need to hear it." It was a demand, but also a request. He would take what he wanted, but only if I gave him me – all of me.

His blue eyes pierced me, saw into the deepest parts of my heart, my mind. He didn't realize he already had what he was asking for. I'd been his for a year, and would be for many, many more.

It was easy to say, because it was true.

I took a breath and gave him what he wanted. "I'm yours."

I was utterly lost to him. Given over to him freely, like the most heartfelt Christmas gift.

"I love you, Anna." He claimed my lips and took me, sliding in hard and sure.

The bells on the Christmas tree began to ring, and kept up a lovely jingle until late in the night.

Bad Boy Valentine

CHAPTER ONE
JESS

I PEERED THROUGH THE peephole as my neighbor shoved his key into the lock of his apartment door. His broad back was covered with a t-shirt even though the weather still carried a winter chill. Tattoos snaked from his sleeves, black ink in stark lines covering all the way to his wrists.

He turned the lock, the click loud in the quiet hallway. I let out a breath. He froze. Then he turned his head, looking right at me over his shoulder. I already knew his eyes were a deep green. I'd spied on him before, more times than I'd like to admit.

My skin tingled as he eyed the peephole. I didn't dare move. If I did, he might know I was there. My palms began to sweat where they rested against the door as the moment lasted, his gaze watchful. Finally, he smirked the slightest bit, his full lips quirking before he turned and pushed through his door. He slammed it behind him and I backed away and rubbed my hands down my pajama pants.

Holy shit. Did he know I was there? I'd watched him for months, ever since he'd moved in right at Thanksgiving.

But I was always careful, never meeting his eye on the few occasions when we'd passed in the hall or the lobby. I was far too shy to ever really look at him, much less speak to him.

I turned and took the few steps to my couch before sinking down and dragging my laptop over. I went to his Twitter, wondering if he'd posted anything new in the past hour. Nothing. I drummed my short nails on the computer before clicking over to his Instagram. There were two new photos – both models he'd no doubt been shooting for the morning. They were perfect, lying on a bed in their bras and panties while staring lustfully at the camera.

Looking down at my curvy frame, completely devoid of ink or anything extraordinary, I realized for the millionth time that I didn't have a chance with Michael. He was chiseled and lean, with dark hair and deep green eyes. His pierced eyebrow and motorcycle only added to his mystique. He was intensely gorgeous, untouchable. More than that, he was an artist with a bigtime reputation for his ability to take amazing photos. Not to mention, he had a dark past. My past was boring and would likely put a man like Michael Williams to sleep.

The lusty models stared back at me, but really, they were staring at Michael, at his amazing body and intelligent eyes. I flipped the laptop closed and leaned back, glaring at the ceiling and trying to shake my obsession with my neighbor. It hadn't worked yet.

I checked my phone. *Shit.* I was going to be late for class. I darted up and went to my bedroom, throwing on a v-neck long sleeved t-shirt, jeans, and some tall boots. After brushing my teeth and hair, I grabbed my jacket and messenger bag.

I barreled out my door, slammed it closed, and turned to lock it.

"Hi."

I looked up slowly, the hair on the back of my neck standing at attention. He was behind me. Michael was in the hall. Behind me. Talking to me. *Oh my god.* I stared at my door, frozen to the spot. How long had he been standing there? Seconds, minutes, hours? I had no idea. I forced myself to breathe.

"Are you okay?" A smile was in his voice.

I focused on the peephole. I was on the wrong side of it.

"I-I . . ."

"What's you name?" The floorboard creaked behind me.

"My name?" Fog swirled around my brain.

He chuckled, a low sound that made my stomach clench. "Yeah, what's your name?"

"Jess." I wanted to turn and look at him, but I couldn't. I already knew every line of his face, his neck, his arms. But what would he think if he saw all of me?

"Short for something?"

Did he just call me short? "What?"

The floorboard creaked again and his shadow fell against the wall next to me.

"I mean, is your full name Jessica?"

"Yes." I swallowed hard and turned my head toward him, even though I knew it was a mistake.

"I'm Michael."

I know. He moved so he leaned against the wall next to my door, his broad chest taking up every bit of real estate my eyes could see. I looked up, past his adam's apple, the tip of his chin, his full lips, and aquiline nose until I was looking into his eyes. They sparkled as if with some private joke. He was laughing at me, just like I'd feared.

I dropped my eyes and frowned at my plain clothes and my body. Then I turned on my heel before striding away to the elevator. I may not have been a model, but I had some pride left.

"Wait." His voice radiated confidence, a tantalizing smile still woven into the sound.

I sped my pace and stabbed the down button on the

elevator. I could feel him behind me, following me at a leisurely pace like the killer in a slasher flick. He stopped a few paces at my back.

"Where's the fire, *Jess*?" He put a hiss at the end of my name that had heat bursting in my cheeks.

"I'm late." My voice came out more harshly than I intended. I just wanted to escape him, to get behind my door and watch him, to follow his social media, to dream about his body, his mouth. I wanted my fantasy Michael to stay firmly in place, because I knew the real Michael would never be interested in me.

"For what?" He took a step nearer. I could feel his body heat against my exposed neck. He was close, too close.

"Class."

"Do you pay as close attention in class as you do around here?" He was right behind me.

I trembled at his nearness, at the scent of his aftershave, at the deep growl of his voice. I was afraid and wanting and anxious and desperate for him all at once.

"I don't know what you mean." I knew exactly what he meant. He must have seen me watching him.

"I think you do."

Where is the elevator?

"I-I don't." Was that my breathy voice?

"I watch people for a living, Jess. I see them, everything about them, and then I capture them." His voice lowered and I could feel his breath whisping through the dark brown strands of hair covering my ear. "Would you like to be captured?"

He was ... *He was coming onto me?* My body was on fire. I turned to him, his gaze bearing down on me like a weight. My heart had long since run away, the beat far too fast to stay put. A five o'clock shadow graced his angular jaw and the eyebrow piercing caught the light.

His eyes were flecked with a lighter hazel and his dark brows were drawn down, as if he were concentrating. I swallowed thickly when it became clear he was concentrating on my lips.

The elevator dinged. I hurried inside and turned around to face him again, something inside me screaming that putting my back to him was a mistake. He put a hand up, holding the doors open and putting the expansive ink of his full sleeve on display. I would have loved to follow the pattern, memorize every line, but I couldn't escape his gaze.

There was no air, not even a puff of it, anywhere near me. Those green eyes pinned me until I backed into the steel wall, my chest rising and falling rapidly. The doors started buzzing, as if irritated by his interference. He didn't move, just let his gaze rove slowly down my body and back up before focusing on my eyes with an intensity I'd never seen in anyone.

He smirked and backed away.

The doors moved together in slow motion. "Don't be late to class, Jess. I'll see you when you get back." His words flowed around me and then I was sinking.

CHAPTER TWO
JESS

CLASS WAS HAPPENING. THE professor was talking, my classmates were answering, and there was a general hum of note-taking on keyboards and the scratch of pencils or pens on paper.

I wasn't there. I was still in the hallway on the fourteenth floor, standing with Michael at my back. His voice whispering darkly in my ear. Heat coursed through my body at the memory and I shifted in my seat, the tingle between my legs demanding some sort of movement.

"Ms. Shakoor?" Professor Ball asked.

"What?" I looked down to him from the fifth row of the classroom's stadium seating.

"You volunteered, did you not? So, what's the answer?" His glasses were slightly askew as he looked up at me.

"I volunteered?" I looked at both of my hands on my laptop keys. I definitely did *not* volunteer.

"I asked whether the tort of negligence carries a two-year or four-year statute of limitations in this state, and you made a sort of a high-pitched grunt." The class snickered around me. "I thought you were volunteering."

I wanted to sink under the table and stay there until class was over, everyone had gone, and the cleaning staff had turned off the lights for the night.

"I apologize. It's two years."

"Correct. Moving on . . ."

His voice faded out as I ducked my head lower, letting my long layers of dark hair hide my bright red face from the people around me. I never volunteered, and I especially did not volunteer by making a sex sound when thinking about Michael. Not that I'd know a sex sound if it bit me on the ass. A vibrator sound? I knew all about that.

Once class was over, I kept my head down and walked two doors down for my next hour-long lecture.

"Oh, and before I forget, Happy Valentine's Day tomorrow everyone," Professor Ball called.

I'd completely forgotten that the holiday was the next day, Saturday. It didn't matter. I intended to stay in and study while making sweet tongue love to a pint of gelato.

It was my last semester in undergrad, and I was wrapping up my pre-law degree. I had already been accepted to law school and intended to get through it in two years instead of the regular three. I was determined to make it, to rise farther and faster than anyone in my family ever dreamed. Not that they would notice or care.

After my last class let out, I headed to the library and finished up my reading for the next week, just like I usually did on Friday nights.

By the time I got back to my apartment, it was almost 11 p.m. I would have stressed about possibly running into Michael again, but he was a night owl. He rarely stayed home once the sun went down.

The elevator slid open and I peered out, making sure the coast was clear. His door was shut and mine beckoned. I crept down the hall and slid my key in the lock, wincing at the clicking sound of metal on metal. But it opened and I darted inside and got it closed without incident.

I dropped my heavy book bag on the floor and stared

through the peephole. *Was he there?* The hallway stayed solemn, quiet. Not a sound and no movement from across the hall. He was gone for the night.

I let out a sigh of relief and disappointment all mixed into one. It was a good thing he was gone. That little hallway interlude had been so strange. My nipples hardened at the thought and my imagination started adding more to what happened.

"I want you." Michael staring at me, his green eyes so luminous.

"I want you, too." I drop my book bag and wrap my arms around his neck.

He lifts me up, his hands on my ass as he pushes me back against the wall before kissing down my neck.

"You're so hot, Jess. I've never seen a woman more beautiful than you." He says against my skin.

"Prettier than the models?"

"What models?"

I smiled and let my hand trail down to my jeans.

"Oh, Michael, make love to me."

"Are you sure?" He whispers in my ear.

"Yes."

"I'll be gentle." He pulls me from the wall and carries me to his apartment. "The first time."

"God, yes." I moan.

"You like it rough, baby?" He opens his door and takes me through his tastefully decorated living room into his bedroom with the mirrors on the ceiling and the black comforter on the bed.

I unbuttoned and unzipped my pants, pushing my fingers down into my panties and against my clit. It was already buzzing, ready to blow. I moaned lightly.

"Yes, please."

"You want me to hurt you?"

"Yes." I breathe.

"Good." He throws me onto the bed and pulls his shirt over his head, showing me his miles of ink.

His cock is hard against his jeans, the outline thick and threatening. He unbuttons his fly and pushes them down far enough that I can get a look at it. It looks like . . .

I closed my eyes harder and kept working my clit as my sighs escaped and grew louder.

He grips the base and strokes down the length. His cock is beautiful. It looks . . .

I pulled my hands from my jeans and bounced my head against the door. I'd only ever seen dicks on the Internet. Never in person. For some reason, not being able to truly picture his was like a cold shower right then. But the figurative water did nothing to cure my burning need for Michael.

I replayed the scene in the hallway over and over again in my mind. He asked if I wanted to be captured, but did that mean take my photograph, or did it mean more? I hoped more, so much more. But no matter how much I wanted him, I was a coward. Any resolve at finally popping my cherry would fail, and I would run back to my apartment. I would keep watching, lusting, and dreaming about Michael. *Jess, you are pathetic.*

"But I want him so fucking bad." I bounced my head on the door again as my words shot loud in my quiet apartment. "Why are you so hot, Michael? Why?"

I shook my head, willing myself to get my shit together. I would do what I did every night. Have some fun with my vibrator while I imagined Michael pounding me from behind and pulling my hair.

After letting out a deep sigh, I turned around and peered through the peephole again.

I squealed and my knees went weak. Michael was standing right outside, no doubt having heard every crazy word I'd just said to myself.

CHAPTER THREE
MICHAEL

I SHOULDN'T HAVE. I knew it, but when I'd felt her eyes on me that afternoon, I couldn't take anymore. I'd approached her. Finally. I asked her name. I already knew it – Jess Shakoor. I asked her about her classes. I already knew about those, too. There was very little I hadn't been able to learn about my shy neighbor. She was my obsession. I'd taken more photos of her in the past months than I had of actual models at my shoots.

I ran a hand over my face as I sat in the chair near my door and waited for her to return that night. It was late for her, though not for me, when near-silent footsteps sounded in the hallway. She was being quiet, but I heard her key in the lock.

I rose quietly and watched her ease inside her apartment. She dressed demurely in baggy t-shirts and ill-fitting jeans. But I knew what was underneath. Her plump ass haunted my fantasies and her large, round tits were made for my palms.

I couldn't help the smirk that turned the corner of my mouth. She thought she was slick, thought I didn't see her watching me for the past few months. Of course I knew.

What she didn't know was that I was watching her, too. I knew where she was from, who her parents were, what she was studying, and that she'd been accepted to law school. I knew everything, except the one thing that I wanted most.

I wanted to know what she tasted like.

My cock hardened at the thought of finally getting a little bite of Jess. I opened my door and went to hers. There was no plan. I was going to knock, introduce myself a bit more cordially and then ... *What? What would I do?* I wanted to barge in, throw her on the bed, and fuck her. But that was frowned upon, generally speaking.

I looked down and realized I wasn't wearing a shirt, just some gym shorts. I couldn't knock on her door like this. I was about to take a step back when I heard her voice. Or rather, heard her exhales and a low keening sound. I moved closer, putting my eye to her peephole. There was nothing except some dark strands of hair. She must have been leaning against the door.

The sound came again. This time it was definitely a throaty moan. My cocked kicked to attention as I pressed my ear to the door. It was as if I could feel her heartbeat vibrating through the wood.

"Yes, please." The lightest whisper from her side.

My palms were hot against her door, and I eyed the handle. Had she locked it?

"But I want him so fucking bad." Her voice was desperate. And then there was a knocking sound, as if she were hitting the back of her head against the door. "Why are you so hot, Michael? Why?"

That was it. The end for me. I had to have her. There was no turning back.

"Jess?" I asked.

A sharp intake of breath and then silence.

"Jess, let me in." I was going crazy just imagining her on the other side of the door, her eyes wide, her fear something I could taste.

The lock clicked over. *Shit.*

I leaned in closer, so I was looking right at her through the peephole. "Jess, I know what you were doing in there. I know you were thinking about me."

I was so hot and my cock so hard that it was already leaking precum at the thought of getting inside her.

"I was just . . ." Her voice was shaky.

"Were you touching yourself?"

"I . . ."

"Don't lie, Jess. I'll know if you do." I ran my hands up the cool wood, tension in every one of my muscles that demanded I break down the door and take what I wanted.

"Yes." So soft I almost missed it.

"Then open the door for me. I can make you feel good, Jess. My tongue, my hands, my dick. I'll make you come as many times as you'll let me."

A moan and the same knocking sound came through the wood.

"Just open the door, Jess. I'll show you."

"I can't." She sounded tormented, as if she'd cry on the last syllable.

"Why not?"

"Because I've never. I, um, I've never done anything like what you just said."

Holy shit. I focused my eyes on the peephole, knowing her light blue eyes were looking back at me. "You're a virgin?"

Silence. *Fuck.* I was twenty-seven and bedded more than my fair share, but I'd never in my life had sex with a virgin. Jess was twenty-three, so she'd been waiting a long time. I couldn't stop the smile that took over my lips. I would be her first time, gladly.

"Let me in." I stared harder at the peephole.

"I can't."

"You can." I tried my best to school my features, but I was hungry for her. "Just open the door. I'll handle the rest."

"I'm scared." Her voice softened even more.

75

I snapped out of it the slightest bit. She was afraid. Of course she was afraid. I leaned back, though it took every bit of strength I had. I was going to get through her fucking door tonight or die trying.

"I'm sorry. Look." I held my hands up, palms facing her, and hoped she didn't notice my raging erection. "I don't want to hurt you. I'm sorry I'm coming on strong."

"No, I like it." Her voice was still muffled, but stronger.

That sent my head spinning. *Then why won't you open the door?*

"What can I do, Jess? What can I do to convince you to let me in?"

CHAPTER FOUR
JESS

HE STARED AT ME pensively. My eye was strained from looking through the peephole at him so hard. He wasn't wearing a shirt and an intricate burst of black roses clung to his ribs and disappeared around to his back. He had plenty of other ink, but the roses were my favorite so far.

"Anything. Just tell me. I'll do it." He put his hands behind his head and laced his fingers together like he was about to be arrested. It wouldn't have been his first time. He'd been to prison for a few months when he was younger for stealing photography equipment. It cemented his bad boy reputation and, along with his good looks and smarts, catapulted him to the top of the photography world.

I tapped my fingernails on the door as I considered him. I wanted to open the door, to let him in, to finally give up the piece of me that I'd been saving. My pussy was already wet, my panties sticking to me. I'd been breathing hard from the moment I'd seen him standing outside. Even so, I was afraid.

"Have you ever been naked with a man, Jess?" He dropped his hands to his hips and hooked his thumbs into his shorts.

Oh, god. "N-no."

He smiled, his even white teeth perfect despite the low light of the hallway. "Have you ever seen a dick that was hard because you made it that way? A dick that was ready just for you?"

I scissored my thighs against each other, trying to stem the buzz in my clit. It only made it worse, the sensation heightening each time I moved.

"No."

"Would you like to?"

I examined his broad chest, down the rippling expanse of his abs, and to the long, hard length in his black gym shorts. I'd fantasized about it for so long that seeing it might make me go up in flames. But I wanted it all the same. "You'd do that? Right now? Right there in th-the hall?"

His smile widened. "I'd rather do it on the other side of the door with you there, your eyes watching me, your hands itching to touch me. But as it is, I'll take what I can get. Do you want to see what you do to me?"

Fuck yes. I leaned back and took a breath, my lungs filling but still burning with the need for him.

"Yes." I kept my voice as even as I could, but it still wavered. I was safe here, a door and a deadbolt between him and me. But my voice wasn't trembling from the fear, it was from the excitement.

"I was hoping you'd say that." He eased his shorts down.

I moved up onto my tiptoes and stared hard at each centimeter of his skin that came into view. The fabric caught on the head of his cock. He paused, his deep green eyes still on mine though he couldn't see me.

"Ready?"

Was he teasing me? I put a hand in my hair and pulled, just to feel something other than the out of control lust that was flooding my system. It only made it worse because in my mind it was *his* hand in my hair, *his* inked fingers twisting and pulling the strands until I said his name.

"Michael, yes."

He pushed the waistband out and down. I held my breath as his taut flesh appeared. His head was glistening. I swallowed hard. He kept going until the entire smooth shaft was revealed. It was thick, thicker at the base than the tip, and long. I had never seen a more beautiful cock. I ran my nails down the door.

"You like?" He moved a hand to it and fisted himself.

I moaned and bit my lip to stifle the sound. I didn't like. I *loved.*

I put one hand back into my panties and eased my fingers between my slick folds to my clit. He stroked himself, one slow pump, and I pressed into my nub, sending pleasure flittering across my skin. A high, breathy sound escaped me as I did it.

"Jess?" He stepped closer and I had to get up higher on my toes to see his gorgeous cock. "Are you touching yourself?"

"No." I lied and flicked my fingers over my sweet spot.

"I know you are."

"Mm." I put my hot forehead on the cool door as he came closer, so close I couldn't see his hand anymore. Would I open the door if he asked again? "Maybe."

"Quick question, Jess. Have you seen my piercings?"

"Yes." I delved my fingers lower and brought my wetness out.

"Have you seen my tongue piercing?"

"What?" My breath hitched.

"My tongue is pierced. Any idea how pleasurable that is on your pussy, Jess? How nice it feels on your clit?"

He was so close, like the big bad wolf at my door, demanding I let him in.

I put my free hand on the deadbolt. I put the slightest bit of pressure on it. All I had to do was turn it, and he'd be inside.

"Let me in, Jess." His words were smooth, his voice like slippery silk.

"But I don't even know you." I was surprised at the little piece of logic that escaped my mouth.

"You don't? You haven't been watching me for months right through here?" He tapped at the peephole. "You haven't been to the gallery two blocks over that exhibits my work at least twice a week? You haven't been following my Twitter or Instagram, LegalJ87?"

Shit. I was so busted. He knew about all of it.

"I also follow the tabloids. I saw you with a model on each arm just last month at a New Year's thing." I slapped my hand over my mouth. *Stalker, much?*

"Yeah." He shrugged. "I didn't fuck them, if that's what you're implying. I haven't touched a woman since I moved in here and saw you. You would know. Have you ever seen me bring a woman home?"

I hadn't. I'd often wondered about why he never had company. Then again, he was out all night most of the time. "When you're out at night, you don't . . ."

"Sleep around?" He ran a hand through his hair, mussing his dark fauxhawk. "I have. I did. A lot. I don't make any bones about my past. I've made plenty of mistakes. I've been with women, a lot of them. But I haven't since you, Jess. I swear. Not since I first saw you."

"Why?" My chest was warm, as if filled with steam after each of his revelations.

"You." He shrugged as if that was all he needed to say.

I moved my hand back to the deadbolt.

"Me? Me what?"

"The second I saw you, even though you were too shy to look at me, much less speak to me, I wanted you. I had to have you. I've given you space, Jess. But today, I just couldn't bear it. I need you." He put both hands on my door, the passion in his eyes boring into me. "Now let me in."

I started to flip the bolt.

"But there's one thing you should know, Jess."

My fingers hesitated. "What?"

"Once you let me in there, I'm going to take everything you have, every way that I want. You're mine. I need you to know that."

My heart stuttered and kicked into an even faster beat. Was I ready for this? Could I handle the bad boy from across the hall?

He stared me down with his green gaze flecked with hazel. Did it matter anymore whether I *could* do it? No, it didn't. What I wanted was right in front of me. I realized I was going to do it no matter what.

I took a deep breath and unlocked the door.

CHAPTER FIVE
MICHAEL

I TURNED THE HANDLE and pushed the door open. She'd backed away, her eyes wide as I walked into her home and closed the door behind me with finality.

I stilled for a moment and just looked at her, drinking in her pale smooth skin, heart-shaped face, dangerous curves, and pink lips. My cock roared back to life, and I was no longer content just to look. Rushing to her, I kissed her hard.

She may have had boyfriends in the past, dickless wonders who weren't good enough for her, who would never be the man she needed. But I knew they never kissed her like this, like they couldn't live without her. I teased my tongue along her lips, but she didn't open. She was still shy, even now.

I put a hand in her hair and finally felt the dark strands between my fingers. I gripped close to her scalp and pulled enough for her to know I meant it. She gasped and it was just the opening I needed. I darted my tongue inside and finally got a full taste of what was mine.

She was a good six inches shorter than me, so it wasn't difficult to pull her head back at an angle and slant my mouth over hers. She opened all the way, giving herself over to me. I growled my satisfaction into her mouth as she started to move her tongue against mine in tentative strokes.

Her nipples were hard beneath her t-shirt and her large tits were pressed against my chest. I was in heaven as I licked her tongue. She moaned and gripped at the bare skin of my back, her nails digging in just enough to scratch the surface.

She was soft and warm, and I needed her naked. I reached down to her ass and lifted her so she straddled me. Her apartment was a mirror image of mine, so I turned to the right and took her to the bedroom. I didn't break our kiss, needing her mouth, her breath like I need air in my lungs.

I didn't look, just kept walking until my knees bumped into something that must have been her bed. I got on my knees and fell on top of her, her soft body molding to my hard one. My cock was against the heat of her cunt, the juncture of her thighs like the surface of the sun. I needed all of it, no barriers.

Pushing up from her, I grabbed a fistful of her shirt and pulled her to a sitting position.

"Hey!" Her lips were bruised, her eyes dazed. So fucking sexy.

I gripped the hem and yanked the fabric up, forcing her to raise her arms as I pulled the shirt away. She wore a simple white bra, the cups some sort of molded material that I didn't give two shits for.

"Bra off now."

"I don't know if we should—"

"Take it off or I'm ripping it off. Choice is yours."

Fear sparked in her eyes and then a heat that I'd hoped existed under her demure façade. She kicked her chin up a notch in challenge. I smiled. She was a wildcat. She just didn't know it until that moment.

She didn't move, so I gripped the fabric between her

breasts and ripped it away. The bra was a ruin as I pulled it from her and tossed it to the floor. Her breasts were free, and the momentum I had to completely strip her ceased. All I could see were the two tear drop mounds with erect nipples pointing right at me, begging to be in my mouth.

I pushed her back roughly and palmed one while I tongued the other. I groaned against her, the taste of her skin smooth and sweet. Opening my mouth wide, I took as much of her in as I could. Her nipple teased against my tongue, and I slid it out and snared it between my teeth.

She moaned and arched into me as I bit down on her, my hand kneading her other breast. Her hands were in my hair, her nails digging into my scalp as I sampled her. I switched, getting a taste of both before kissing down her stomach. Her skin trembled beneath me, soft and taut at the same time.

I grazed my teeth around her belly button and down to the waist of her jeans. They were half zipped from what she'd been doing earlier behind the door. The memory of her soft sighs had me ravenous. I gripped the jeans at her hips and yanked, pulling them and her panties down in a smooth jerk. She yelped.

"Fuck, Jess." It was all I could say once I saw her glistening slit. It was perfect with a light covering of damp curls.

With her knees still together, I dug the tip of my tongue into the top of her cleft. She bucked, but I gripped her hips hard so she couldn't escape me. I would never let her go, not now that I finally had a taste.

"No one's ever done this to you before?" I asked and ran my tongue even deeper, grazing her clit.

She squealed. "No, never!"

Pride swelled inside me that she'd given *me* this gift. And no one else would ever taste the sweetness I just found. Every last bit of it was mine.

I ripped her jeans and panties the rest of the way down and kissed her ankle, up her calf, her knee, and finally up the creamy expanse of her thigh. When I got close to her wet pussy, I forced myself to work up her other leg first. She deserved the full treatment, and I wanted to sample every last bit of her skin. When I was done, there wouldn't be a place on her body that didn't bear the brand of my mouth.

As I slowly kissed back up her other leg, she let out a series of high moans with each breath. I loved her sounds. I was going crazy to bury my face in her, but I slowed down and pushed her thighs apart.

When met with faint resistance, I growled, "Spread your legs."

She relaxed and gave herself up to me. My big hands looked hot as fuck against her smooth, perfect thighs. She whimpered as I spread her further and breathed on her pussy. Her pink folds were understated and covered in her honey. I was starving for it.

"You afraid, Jess?" I played my tongue over her, barely touching her plump flesh.

She squirmed and dug her hands into my scalp. "No."

"Do you want this?" I ghosted my tongue along her again. Her hips lifted to me but I backed away. I wanted her to tell me, though denying myself was making my cock painfully hard.

"Yes." Barely a whisper.

"Tell me, Jess. Use the words. Tell me exactly what you want." I darted my tongue against her clit, and it took everything I had to stop myself from fastening my mouth to her.

"I want you t-to—"

I moved my palms closer to her pussy and massaged the sensitive skin in the hollow of her thigh. "What, baby? Tell me what."

I wanted her wild. I wanted the shy girl who wouldn't meet my eyes gone. I wanted this wildcat in her place. I licked with just a bit more pressure, teasing against her clit.

She moaned. "I want you to eat my pussy and make me

come."

Her words were like a shot of pure adrenaline, and I couldn't hold back anymore.

CHAPTER SIX
JESS

MY EYES ROLLED BACK in my head as an explosion of sensation rocketed up from my pussy. Michael had teased me into a frenzy but now the tease was over. His mouth was hot and his tongue was as nimble as it was wicked. I used to think that nothing on earth could feel better than a vibrator. I was wrong. So wrong.

He licked from my entrance to my clit in several long strokes and I couldn't stop the moans that welled up inside me. His mouth was electric and I jumped at every touch. His hands were spread along my inner thigh, spreading me so that I was wide open to him.

When he licked up and seized on my clit, I thought I might come off the bed. And then, right when I thought it couldn't get any better, I felt a hard nub of hot metal teasing at my skin.

"Michael!" I gasped as his tongue piercing rake against my clit.

He moved his hands beneath my thighs and pushed my legs so they wrapped around his head. Then his hands snaked up my stomach and gripped my breasts. He groaned into my pussy and my hips rose up even higher, my ass off the bed as he licked and sucked at my most tender spots.

My stomach was already drawn tight as a piano wire when he pinched my nipples hard.

"Oh my god, Michael." It came out in a garble, matching the thoughts that swirled in my head.

When he stabbed his tongue deep into me, any last thought disappeared. I was nothing more than a burning pyre of need. The sensation was foreign but more delicious than anything I'd ever felt.

He moved back to my clit, sucking it between his teeth and rubbing the stud in his tongue over it. I rocked my hips against his mouth, my need overcoming any embarrassment at what I was doing. I had to come. I had to.

"Mmm," he said against me as I rocked harder and harder.

He gripped each breast hard and ran his thumb over my nipples, sending tiny explosions through me and making my pussy tighten. I was close, so close, and when I looked down and saw his eyes fixed on mine, I was gone.

I came on a scream, his name all I could think as my body seized and he kept licking me. My pussy convulsed in the strongest orgasm I'd ever experienced. Wave after wave of bliss washed over me as the pleasurable waves multiplied until I was awash in a sea of indulgence. He never stopped licking, his groans vibrating into me as I arched off the bed. As I came back down, I relaxed my legs and gulped in huge breaths of air.

He gave me a few more licks, each one sending a tremor through my hypersensitive body. Then he stood and pushed his shorts off. His cock was so thick that I swallowed hard. But, god, he was gorgeous. His wide chest tapered to washboard abs, a trim waist, and that perfect length.

"This is yours, Jess." He gripped himself as he held my gaze. "All of this." He pumped slowly, his hand sliding along the skin where I wanted my mouth to be. "Is yours."

I raised up on my elbows, my legs still spread, my body completely open to him. I was ready. "I want it. Give it to me." Was that my raspy sex voice demanding his cock?

His eyes lit at my words and climbed on top of me, kissing up my stomach and between my breasts to my mouth. He licked across my lips and I opened for him as our mouths met. I tasted myself on him and felt his shaft against my hot, wet skin.

Right at that moment, I realized I may have asked for more than I could handle. His cock was so hard and big that I wondered how it would ever fit inside me. He swiped his tongue over mine and tangled his fingers in my hair before pulling my head back onto the bed. His lips moved to my neck where he sucked my skin between his teeth and nipped at me.

I dug my nails into his back and exhaled hard. He laughed against my skin and kissed to my ear. "I know you want my cock."

I moaned as he pinned my earlobe between his teeth.

"I know you want it deep inside you. Do you want me to come in you? I already know the answer." He thrust his hips against me, his head rubbing sinfully against my clit. "You want it all, don't you? I bet you can't wait for me to fill every hole you've got. My little virgin slut."

His words should have angered me, should have had me questioning him. They had the opposite effect. Dirty talk turned me the fuck on. I melted beneath him, my fear draining away as desire roared up into its place. I wanted everything he offered.

"That's what I thought." He gripped my throat and licked up my ear. "I know you want it hard. I know you want me to make it hurt."

"Yes." I moaned as he squeezed my neck. He read my thoughts, my deepest needs, my darkest wants.

"Spread wide for me." He released my neck and put both hands next to my head, pushing up and away from me.

I did as he said, letting my legs fall wide, my knees bent. The ink on his chest was stark, and I was overcome with the urge to lick every line, every bit of residual pain it took to mark his skin so beautifully. His gaze trailed down my body to my quivering pussy.

"Fuck." His jaw tightened and he moved his hips back and forth, his slick head teasing my clit until I was moving with him. My strokes meeting his and increasing the buzz between my legs.

"I'm going to try to go slow." He shook his head. "I *will* go slow. For your first time." He looked back to my eyes. "But after this, after I've finally sank balls deep inside you, I can't make any more gentle promises. Understand?"

My body thrilled at his threat. "Yes."

His face softened. "It's going to hurt at first, but then I promise I'll make it all better. Trust me?"

I took a deep breath. This was it. The moment I'd been waiting for, the man I'd been lusting for.

I met his gaze. "Take me."

He closed his eyes as if he'd just heard some enticing music. Then he slid his hips back and let the head of his cock fall to my entrance. He looked down to where our bodies touched and pressed forward.

Pressure and then nothing. He stopped.

"Fuck, you're tight, Jess." His biceps trembled as he held himself over me.

"More," I breathed. I wanted to be filled.

He moved into me, stretching me, then he pulled back and pushed in further. A slight pinch and then just the amazing feel of him.

"You okay?" His voice was gruff but controlled.

"Yes. More."

He gritted his teeth, then backed out again and pushed deeper. It stung but I found myself clawing at his shoulders.

"All of it, please. I need it."

At my words he pulled back again and surged forward. I yelped at the sharp ache and then moaned as he settled down on top of me.

"Shit, Jess." His voice was gravelly.

He stilled as my body adjusted to him, to his thick length.

"Still okay?"

"Don't stop." I was desperate for more. I'd finally crossed the threshold. Now it was time to explore.

"I have to go slow." His voice was a mix of pleasure and pain as he looked into my eyes.

"Please, give it to me." I moved my hips against his, getting a taste for the friction that had my body spiraling even higher.

He groaned and buried his head in the crook of my neck. "I want to pin your knees at your ears and fuck you until you scream. But I can't. Not this time."

"This time. Every time. I'm begging you." I clutched his hair and arched my back.

Slowly, he pulled out and pushed back in. Then he did it again, faster.

"Yes." My breasts rubbed against him as he rocked into me, my nipples aching for his touch.

He bit my shoulder and started a slow rhythm, giving me just enough to stoke the fire without sending me up in flames. He ground against my clit on each stroke as I met him. I didn't know it would feel like this. He was all around me, inside me, ingrained in every cell of my body.

He took my mouth, his tongue stabbing into me in the same rhythm as his cock. I angled my head so he could go even deeper. He growled and sped his pace, finally giving in to what he wanted instead of fearing hurting me. *Yes.*

I lifted my hips, relishing every second of wet contact. He pistoned into me again and again, each pump harder than the last, until the sounds of skin on skin ricocheted around the room. Our bodies, slick with sweat, slid against each other as he broke our kiss and fisted my hair, pulling my head to the side.

His teeth in my neck had my body tightening even more, my pussy clenching him even deeper inside me. His movements grew wilder, and I wrapped my arms around his neck. So much delicious friction made the pleasure pool between my legs.

"I'm close, Michael."

"Fucking hell." He shoved into me harder, the headboard banging against the wall. "Come on my cock. I want to feel every last jolt in your sweet pussy."

He bit down harder at my throat. I angled my hips up to him so every thrust hit my clit. I was already there. I clenched and my muscles seized as my pussy writhed around his cock, squeezing and caressing him as I came on a wave of sweet release.

He grunted, deep and masculine, and he pushed as far as he could go.

"Oh, fuck Jess. Fuck." His words were muffled against my neck, but I felt his cock kicking inside me.

The thought of him coming kept my orgasm rolling, like a never-ending wave on the shore. I didn't realize I'd been saying his name like a chant until I came back down. I stopped my mouth, though my heart galloped ahead, beating out of my chest.

It was over. Michael had taken my virginity.

CHAPTER SEVEN
MICHAEL

I COULDN'T BELIEVE I'D just taken her virginity. And done it far more roughly than I'd intended. I winced at the thought of hurting her.

She sighed beneath me and lazily ran her fingers in my hair.

"Did I hurt you?" I lifted my head to look into her eyes, dreading I would see pain in them.

She nodded and bit her lip. "Yes. Can we do it again?"

I laughed and put my palm on her cheek. "As many times as you want."

She grinned and my heart, which was already beating rapidly, sped up. She was radiant, her skin pinked from her exertions and her eyes a sparkling blue. I kissed her, gently this time, and savored her taste. I wanted to stay inside her, but I wasn't sure what was in store for her since she'd been a virgin.

I backed away slowly and looked down. I quirked my head to the side. No blood or anything dramatic. I looked back up to her, and she was peering down, too, no doubt looking for the same thing I was.

She smiled and lay back. "Good. I read it's different for

everyone."

I moved back on top of her and kissed her before resting my forehead on hers. "How was it for you?"

She looked up, pretending to give it some deep thought. "I would say it was . . . hmm . . . Let me think—"

I bit her bottom lip and pulled it into my mouth.

"Mmm." She ran her hands through my hair. "It was better than I ever imagined."

Pride roared to life inside my chest. I had given her a great first time. I wanted to get up and strut around the apartment complex. Fuck that, the block.

She ran her hand down to my cheek and cupped it. I leaned into her light touch.

"So, what happens now?" she asked.

"Now." I dropped another kiss on her lips before getting to my feet. "I bring you some tissues, we clean up, then you come over to my place for a late night snack."

I went to her bathroom and smiled at all the girly items on the counter – face creams, lotions, and hair products. Then I took her the tissue and helped her clean up.

Pulling on my shorts, I looked at her over my shoulder. "Wear PJs. You're spending the night."

Her eyebrows went up as I walked out. She shouldn't have been surprised. When I'd said she was mine, I'd meant it. I knew from the moment I'd first seen her that she was something special, something that I had to have. The more I learned about her, the more I knew it was true. Love at first sight. I didn't think it was remotely possible until the day I'd seen her, the day I'd finally laid eyes on the one made for me. And then I was a believer.

I went to my apartment kitchen and, after turning the sound system on low, started making some peanut butter and jelly sandwiches, midnight snack of champions. I glanced over to the clock. It was only five more minutes until midnight. Until Valentine's day. I smiled. I'd never had a "Valentine" before. Never kept a girl around long enough to indulge in the holiday with her. But with Jess? I was going to go all out on romance. I wish I'd planned it better, but I wouldn't change the way it went down for a second.

When I was finishing up with the last one, I heard my door open.

"Michael?" Her voice, but now shot through with shyness.

Her hesitant movements had me smirking and my cock hardening. I would bring the wildcat back out, and sooner rather than later. "Come in and lock it behind you."

"Okay." The lock clicked over and she padded into my galley kitchen.

I almost dropped the butter knife. She wore a tank top, no bra, and her nipples were hard enough to cut glass. On the bottom, a set of shorts with lace around the edges. It was a matching set, and I wanted it matching in a torn heap on the floor.

She fidgeted under my stare and crossed her arms over her chest.

"No." I was on her in the blink of an eye, one hand in her hair and the other pushing her arms down. "I want to see you."

She gasped and stared up at me, her guileless eyes bright. Slowly, she let her arms fall.

I backed away and took my time looking her over. She was a curvy hourglass. Her long, dark hair draped over her shoulder and her mouth was the perfect pout. There must have been countless men who'd tried for her. I stood a little straighter knowing she'd saved herself and given it all to me.

"Do you have any idea how gorgeous you are?" I wanted to get my camera out right then and there. But it could wait. I had to taste her again first.

She blushed and dropped her gaze. "No."

I put my index finger under her chin and lifted her eyes back to mine. "I have never seen anything more beautiful."

"But you photograph models all day . . . Or all night, I

guess."

"Those girls don't hold a candle. And they certainly don't hold my interest." I used to date models. They were easy and available. Not anymore.

I leaned in and brushed my lips across hers. She closed her eyes and tilted her head back for me. I ran my hand down her throat, to her collar bone, and then lower to her breast. It was somewhat more than a handful, firm and yet still soft. Perfect.

Her stomach growled, and she opened her eyes. "Sorry. I skipped dinner."

I didn't want to let her go, but more important than my need to claim her was my need to take care of her.

"You came to the right place. Have a seat."

"Those look good." She gestured to the sandwiches with a graceful movement. "I'm starving."

I poured two glasses of milk, and we sat at the small bar.

"So," she said in between bites, "I know a few things about you, but not everything. Do you do this a lot?"

"What? Seduce virgins?"

She snorted. "Um, no. I guess I meant have sleepovers with strange women?"

"No. Like I said, I make no bones about my past. I've been with a lot of women."

She flinched a little at my words. I took her hand and pressed it between mine.

"But that was before you."

"You don't know me." She shook her head.

"At the risk of sounding like a total stalker, I know you're about to go to law school. I know you worked your way through undergraduate. I know your parents have never really supported you and that everything you've done, you've done on your own. You've been on Dean's List every semester. You volunteer at the Humane Society even though you're allergic to cats. I could go on but I don't want you to run out the door."

She put her glass of milk down. "How do you know all that?"

My stomach twisted. I didn't want her to think I was a perv or something. "Social media snooping and, well, I own the building, so I did a background check on you when you moved in."

She stared at me, her mouth slightly open.

"But it's not like I put cameras in your apartment or anything," I hurriedly added. *Had I thought about it?* I plead the Fifth.

"What?" Her eyebrows shot up. "Wait, you own the building?"

I tossed my napkin on the bar and leaned back. "Yeah. Bought it two years ago."

She drank down the rest of her milk, as if buying time to think.

"Tell me what you know about me. Don't hold back. I know you've done your homework, too." I smiled remembering how many times I'd caught her watching me.

"Well, she tucked a lock of hair behind her ear and met my eyes. "I know you have a, um, darker past. That you've been to prison. That you are notorious for getting with models at your shoots—"

"Not anymore," I interjected.

She nodded. "Okay, so you *were* notorious for that. That you're one of the most sought-after photographers in town. That you ride a motorcycle and have a penchant for fast cars. And that you make my heart do this weird stutter step whenever I see you." Her eyes grew wide when she finished her last sentence, and she looked away.

Her honesty was the sweetest thing I'd ever heard.

"I feel it, too."

"You do?" She watched me through her lashes.

"Yes."

"Then what took you so long to-to . . ."

"To talk to you?" I ran my fingers through her hair.

"Yes."

"I had some work to do."

She canted her head to the side. I had to explain, but hated telling her the whole, ugly truth. Still, it had to be done.

"Work on myself, really, is what it amounts to. What you said about the women." I rolled my shoulders, suddenly nervous. "That was true. I didn't want to be that man anymore. I didn't want to get black out drunk or high as a kite after a shoot and wake up with strange women in my bed. That wasn't good enough for you." I took her hands in mine as I laid myself bare. "*I* wasn't good enough for you. The moment I saw you, I knew. I knew it in my bones. I know that sounds crazy, but it's true. I just needed some time to get my shit together."

Her eyes opened wider as I spoke. "For me?"

"All for you. Yes." I kissed her fingertips. "I still shoot at night. But I don't sleep with models. I barely even drink anymore and I haven't touched powder in months. Don't get me wrong, I'm still going to ride my bike. I'm still going to get inked and pierced and probably get into fights. I'm still going to be me, but I want to be the best version of me possible. Because that's what you deserve."

A tear rolled down her cheek and I wiped it away.

"Is it too much?"

She cleared her throat, the tears thick in the sounds. "No." She kissed me, all shyness gone. Her eyelids fluttered closed as she licked my lips and moved her hands to the back of my neck.

She was sweet from her sandwich and cool from the milk. But her body was pure heat. I ran my hands to her waist and edged my fingers under her top. My palms were itching for her skin. Chill bumps erupted along her sides as I moved my hands up to her ribs, pushing the fabric from her as I went.

She kissed down my jaw and licked along the swirl of ink at the side of my neck. I groaned and pulled her to me, her hot cunt straddling my leg. My cock was already back in fighting form, pushing at my shorts and trying to get to the sweet paradise between her thighs.

I pushed her top the rest of the way up and cupped her breasts, running my thumb over the erect tips. She slid her hands down my chest, her fingertips pressing against me and feeling every ridge and ripple as she went. When her fingers reached under the waistband of my shorts at the same time she nipped at my neck, I had to take her hands and pull them away.

"Can you do this again so soon? Because if we keep going like this, I can't stop. I won't." I couldn't be anything but honest with her. I already wavered on the edge of throwing her onto the kitchen floor and fucking her black and blue.

"I want to." She strained against my hold, her fingers seeking my cock.

Fuck. I released her and she reached into my shorts and palmed me. When she made contact, I hissed.

"So that's what it feels like." She smiled.

I let my head loll back as her fingers explored me. Then her mouth was on my nipple, teasing the barbell and running her teeth along the raised skin. My hips jerked as she squeezed my length in her small palm. I refused to come in her hand, but if she didn't stop, I would.

"Come on." I pulled her to me and lifted her under her thighs.

I was almost to my bedroom when a loud bang shattered the relative stillness of my apartment.

"Michael? It's Layla. Want to be my slutty valentine again this year?" Her words were slurred.

Jess tensed in my arms and my heart sank. No matter how much I'd tried to change for her, my past was still there. She pushed against my hands so she could stand up.

I reluctantly let her go.

"It's okay. I'll just . . . I'll just go back to my place." She studied her feet, her dark hair hiding her eyes.

I put my hands on her shoulders. "That's my past.

You're my future. I'm sorry. Please, stay."

"Michael!" Layla called and banged on the door some more. I didn't remember her, not even a little.

"I just can't." She sidestepped me and walked away. I wanted to grab her, to tie her to my bed, to do anything but let her walk away. I didn't. I wanted her to choose me as freely as I'd chosen her.

CHAPTER EIGHT
JESS

HE FOLLOWED ME AND opened the door. The need to escape blotted out any other thought. Jealousy and embarrassment swirled like a cyclone inside me. I hurried past a clearly trashed Layla and into my apartment. I clicked the lock over and whirled to see what he did with the willowy blonde at his door.

"Hey, baby. Didn't know you had company. Want some more?" She slid the spaghetti strap of her top off her shoulder, showing her breast to Michael.

Rage boiled up inside me and I fisted my hands at my sides.

"Stay here." He shut the door in her face.

"Are we playing dominant and submissive games?" she stage-whispered through the door. "I wait out here for you all obedient? I can do that." She laughed and then dropped to her knees and bowed her head.

A raging inferno couldn't have pulled me away from that door. I watched and waited. What was he doing? The waiting gave me time to think, at least. Had I been too hasty in leaving? I wanted him. The way he'd explained changing for me, even though we were almost total strangers. It enthralled me instead of frightened me. He seemed so devoted, but then the model had shown up and rattled me out of the daydream. Had he really changed if a model still showed up at his door and declared herself his "valentine"?

I stared as she played on her phone and leaned against his door.

"Getting a bit chilly out here, love." She rapped her knuckles on the wood.

The elevator dinged. I peered to the right and saw a man approaching.

"Ms. Layla?"

"Yeah?" She got to her feet, though she swayed. "What do you want?"

"I'm Frank, your driver. I was called to come pick you up."

"What?" She banged on Michael's door. "You fucking prick!"

"Please, miss. Allow me to escort you to the car." Frank held his arm out to her as she beat and clawed at Michael's door to no avail. After a few more moments filled with vile curses and a final kick at the unmoving door, she stepped back and smoothed a hand down her long yellow locks.

"Fine. You were a lousy fuck anyway."

She's drunk and *a liar.*

She screamed and gave the door the finger before taking Frank's arm and moving toward the elevator.

I thought I heard Michael's low laughter, but couldn't be sure. Once the elevator dinged and Layla was gone, Michael opened his door and stepped out in the hall.

"I know you're there, Jess." He stared at the peephole, just like before.

"Yes, I am."

"As you can see, I have no interest in anyone else." His earnest green eyes struck right at my soul. "But, I want you to make your own decisions. So, I'm going to leave my door unlocked and go get in my bed. I would love for you to join me. And, not to be hokey here, but I would also love it if you would be my valentine." He tapped the skin over his heart where an intricate lattice heart was inked in sturdy black. "Anyway. I've laid out all my cards. I want you. I ..." He took a deep breath. "I know it sounds impossible, but I love you. From the first moment I saw you, I've loved you."

My heart seemed to stop completely before taking off at a breakneck pace. Did the remarkable man in the hallway just say he *loved* me?

"So, I hope to see you inside." He gave me a panty-melting smile and backed into his apartment.

When he was out of sight, I turned and leaned against my door. I was having trouble catching my breath. He said he *loved* me. I covered my mouth with my hand and squealed into it while jumping up and down like an idiot. Then I actually pinched myself. It hurt. This was real.

I darted to my bathroom and checked myself in the mirror, but I couldn't do much because a smile seemed permanently affixed to my face. *Get it together, Jess.*

Back into the living room and out to the hallway. I put a hand to my chest, as if that could calm my heartbeat, and then swung his door open.

The room was dark. I crept past his cozy décor – nothing liked I'd imagined it before – and only paused to admire a couple of the dozens of photographs he had along his walls. All of them were done by him, and I'd seen versions of them at the gallery a couple of blocks away.

His bedroom door was open. I straightened my back and walked through. There were no mirrors on the ceiling and his bed had a white duvet instead of a black one.

What I saw on the bed made my jaw drop. Michael looking at me with lust in his eyes. His hands were laced behind his head and the white duvet covered just to his hips. He was sex on a platter. His piercings glinted in the light of his lamp and his sculpted body had my mouth watering. His hair was still jutting this way and that from when I'd run my hands through it earlier.

"Come here." His voice was low and full of command.

I couldn't have disobeyed if I'd tried. I walked to him as he sat up and swung his legs off the bed.

"On your knees."

I dropped in front of him and looked up into his eyes.

"Have you made up your mind?" He stroked a hand through my hair.

"Yes. I had it made up the moment I saw you. I want you."

He smiled, devilish and sincere all rolled into one.

I darted my eyes to the duvet covering his cock.

"Curious, Jess?"

Yes, very. After I'd touched it earlier, I wanted it in my mouth. But then Layla had shown up and ruined it.

"Yes. I want to taste it."

A low growl came from his throat and he flexed his fists. "That is the hottest thing I've ever heard in my fucking life."

I grabbed the duvet and pulled it away. He was so hard, his cock darkened and the tip wet. I licked my lips and grabbed it at the base, the same way he'd done in the hallway.

His head fell back. "Fucking wildcat."

I smiled and licked the tip. He jerked in my hand but then stilled again. It was salty on my tongue and I licked again. He looked back down to me and put his hands in my hair.

"Take it."

I didn't need any more encouragement. I opened my mouth wide and slid it in. It was thick on my tongue and I moved too quickly, trying to get as much of it in as possible. I gagged and slid it out.

"Sorry." I blushed.

"Don't be sorry. Your mouth feels fantastic."

Emboldened by his words, I slid the tip past my lips

again and lapped at it with my tongue. His grip tightened in my hair as I licked at him. Moving forward, I took him deeper, the tip just hinting at the back of my throat, but not enough to make me gag again.

"That is—" His words cut off into a groan as I hollowed my cheeks and sucked him while moving back and forth.

I gripped his thighs and kept sucking him in and out, using my tongue to lick him as I went. His hips began to pulse against me in time with my rhythm. My pussy was drenched. This was by far the most erotic thing I'd ever undertaken.

"Look at me, Jess."

I looked up and caught his eye as I bobbed on his cock. His jaw was tight, a vein pulsing in his neck.

When I dug my nails into his thighs and pushed him even farther inside, he ripped me up from the floor on a groan and threw me onto my stomach on the bed.

"What—"

His hands were at my shorts, ripping them down my legs. Then he was between my thighs. His palms were on my hips, pulling me back into him. When his cock hit my wet skin I shuddered.

"Remember what I said about losing control?" He wrapped my hair around his hand and pulled me against him.

"Yes." Electricity thrilled through me as the pinpricks along my scalp increased with his tugs.

"This is it." He pushed his head into my opening and I sucked in a breath between my teeth. I was sore, but the feel of his smooth skin went a long way to soothe the ache.

He stilled and then pushed again, then again until his hips were against my ass and I was completely filled with him. I curled my toes when he pulled out and slammed back into me, a loud slap from where our bodies converged.

Then he moved fast, in and out to a pounding beat that I felt in my clit. My breasts bounced and I had to arch my back as he pulled harder on my hair.

"So fucking tight."

His fingertips dug into my hip and I found myself pushing back into him, relishing his aggression as it washed over me in pleasurable jolts. He leaned over my back and reached beneath me, wrapping his arm up to my shoulder and forcing me into his harsh strokes.

"You like that, don't you Jess? You like being filled with my hard cock. I bet you've fantasized about this." He bit into my shoulder and kissed over the sting. "I know I have."

He kept pounding me, his mouth at my ear and his hand at my shoulder. Then he lifted up and splayed his fingers along my upper back.

"Down. I want this fine ass in the air."

I bent my elbows and lay my head on the bed.

"Look at me." His voice was coated in sex.

I craned my neck, the right side of my face pressed into the bed, so I could see him. His body was covered with a fine sheen of sweat and his muscles were in sharp relief with each hard thrust. He brought two fingers to his mouth and licked them before snaking them beneath my body. When he made contact with my clit, I moaned into the bed. His touch made my pussy clench. Bending over me again, he gripped my hair and used his whole body to thrust into me while his fingers circled my tender nub.

"I want to hear my name when you come, wildcat. Got that?"

I clawed at the duvet as he rocketed into me over and over.

He jerked my hair. "Got that?"

"Yes." I moaned as his fingers increased their pace. I had never felt this much pleasure, didn't even know it was possible.

His grunts grew deeper and his cock somehow got

even harder, rubbing my trembling walls just right as his fingers worked me.

"I'm close."

"I'm there. Come with me." He flicked my clit and we both fell over the edge.

Sparks flared across my vision as a tidal wave of bliss flooded my senses.

"Michael!" It was a harsh cry as everything seized and I gave myself over to him, to every bit of pleasure he gave me.

My pussy contracted and convulsed as the rest of me froze. He was still thrusting in shorter strokes as a deep, masculine sound ripped from his lungs. When stilled, I couldn't feel my fingers or toes because I'd curled them so hard.

He rose up and rested a hand on my ass before giving it a light slap. "Fuck, that was hot."

"Unff," I semi-responded. I was still floating somewhere out in the cosmos.

He reached under me and pulled me up so my back was pressed against his chest.

He dropped sweet kisses up my shoulder and to my ear. I let my head fall back against his shoulder.

"I love you, Jess. Happy Valentine's Day."

EPILOGUE
JESS

Valentine's Day, one year later

"WHAT DO YOU THINK?" Michael asked as he lifted his shirt.

I gasped. "Are you kidding?"

"No." He smirked. "Ink is pretty permanent, wildcat."

"That's a huge like, step." I ran my fingers over the fresh ink above the lattice heart on his chest.

"Moving in was, too."

"True. The penthouse suite was a pretty good lure though." I smiled.

"Nothing but the best for my lawyer-in-training."

I looked around at the sun streaming through the windows, the view for miles, and the comfy décor. He certainly spared no expense, and his art along every wall was a bonus. The nude photos of me in the bedroom still made me blush.

I stared at the new ink on his chest and traced along the curving lines of my own name. He had it done in an elaborate script that was gorgeous against his skin.

"You don't like it?" He raised a pierced eyebrow.

I grinned. "You know I love it."

He dropped his shirt. "Good. Then quit touching it. It stings like a bitch."

I laughed and got on my tiptoes to kiss him. He took my breath away like he always did, sweeping his tongue in my mouth and gripping the nape of my neck. But then he pulled away.

"Speaking of taking steps." He cleared his throat.

"What?"

He fumbled in the pocket of his favorite leather jacket and dropped to his knee in front of me.

I brought my hands to my mouth, shock rolling over my like thunder. "Is this—"

"Jessica Louise Shakoor, will you marry me?" He flipped the box open and a dazzling solitaire set in platinum appeared.

My knees turned to jelly and I sank in front of him.

His brows knit in concern and he put a hand on my elbow to steady me. "Jess, you okay?"

"Yes. I just. I can't. I mean. I don't even . . ."

His face fell, the smile gone and sadness in its place. He pulled his hand back and was about to close the lid.

"No!" I grabbed his wrist.

"Yeah, I got it." He dropped his gaze.

"No, I mean yes!"

"What?" The smile crept back into his eyes, his mouth.

"I meant yes. I was just so shocked but yes, a million times *yes*."

He gripped my ass and scooted me toward him before plucking the ring from the box and placing it on my finger. It just fit.

"I can't believe this." I put my hands on his cheeks, the ring stunning but nowhere near as captivating as his smile, his eyes.

And then his arms were around my waist. He laid me gently back on the floor and stripped off his jacket and then his shirt. My eyes went right to the ink, to the profession of his love for me buried in his skin. I would have licked it if it were healed.

He pulled my jeans off and tossed them before unbuttoning his fly. He nestled between my legs and, in one swift move, impaled me as I squirmed beneath him.

"Let's make this official." He thrust deep into me and I moaned.

"I love you, wildcat." He stared into my eyes, into my soul, and into the future he'd planned for us.

"I love you, too."

Bad Boy Valentine *Wedding*

CHAPTER ONE
JESS

"I DON'T KNOW." I turned this way and that, looking at the dress from every angle.

"It's perfect." My Aunt Carrie clasped her hands together in front of her.

Michael's mother, Evelyn, dabbed at her eyes. She had the same green eyes as Michael, but her hair was an ash blonde with streaks of gray. A beautiful woman, she'd created an equally beautiful son. One I intended to marry in three short months after a three-year engagement.

"That dress was made for you." Evelyn coughed to try and cover her tears. She was a wonderful woman, strong yet gracious.

I tended to agree with her. I had never been in a more luxurious article of clothing. The dress was white lace at the top with a sweetheart neckline, lace shoulders, and low back. The bottom fluffed out with tulle, but not too much. It was part Grace Kelly, part Cinderella. The price tag would have likely made me queasy, but Michael sent his mother along to ensure that I got exactly what I wanted, no matter the price. The sales people had hidden the tags from me when I ventured through the racks.

As much as I wanted Aunt Carrie and Evelyn to love the dress, all I cared about was whether Michael would love it.

The sales associate walked up and pinched his chin between his bright blue fingernails while eyeing me up and down. He snapped his fingers at an assistant behind him. She scurried away and returned with a tiara and veil.

He climbed up onto the white podium and surveyed me in the wide mirror. "This will set it off perfectly." Arranging the tiara in my dark hair, he hooked the veil on as well, and let it float down over my face.

Then he backed away, pinching his chin again as his platinum blond hair fell lazily into one of his eyes. "Magnificent." He nodded.

I stared at myself, ignoring his sales talk, and tried to see myself as Michael would. Just the thought of his green eyes watching me walk down the aisle made my heart speed up. I closed my eyes and let the room fall away right along with the sales associate, my aunt, and Michael's mom.

It was just me in the church, walking toward the man I loved. There, at the end of the aisle, Michael stood and waited for me to arrive. His black tux was perfection on his broad shoulders and narrow waist. I smiled and my imaginary Michael smiled back, pure joy on his handsome face.

I opened my eyes, only then noticing they were teary. "I'll take it."

Aunt Carrie and Evelyn clapped and hugged each other as the sales associate grinned.

"Excellent choice. Absolutely stunning. I'll have Margo begin alterations immediately. We already have your measurements." The sales associate helped me down the two steps to the floor and escorted me to the changing room.

After some help with the clips used to hold the back together, I slid the dress off and donned my skirt suit and pumps. Before I left the room, I trailed my fingers over the lace, still not believing that in a few short months I'd no longer be Jess Shakoor. I'd be Mrs. Michael Williams. The thought made me smile and the tears welled in my eyes again.

The three years since I'd met Michael had flown away, eaten up by law school and his photography career, not to mention our frequent travel and nights of lovemaking. I sighed just thinking about the whirlwind he'd swept me up in that day when he came knocking at my door like a hungry wolf, asking me to let him inside my apartment. I'd let him in and then some, loving every second I spent with him.

I gave the sample dress one more goodbye pat and re-entered the main store area. Evelyn and Aunt Carrie stood.

"I can't believe I found it on our first shopping trip." I smiled as they both embraced me.

Evelyn let go of her tight hold on my neck and smoothed a lock of hair behind my ear. "When something is right, you just know it."

I returned her smile, remembering how Michael and I first met. "I know exactly what you mean."

CHAPTER TWO
JESS

"MMMM." A DELICIOUS SENSATION swirled through me. I was panting, my body drawing tighter even as I slumbered.

My eyes fluttered open, the sun barely peeking through the penthouse blinds. I was on my side and Michael was under the covers, licking my pussy and gently spreading my legs just enough to get his tongue to my clit.

I moaned when he stabbed his stiff tongue inside me. He threw the blanket off and spread my legs all the way, diving onto my pussy like he was at a feast. I squealed as my nipples pearled from the cold air and the deliciousness of his mouth on my most sensitive flesh.

I dug my hands into his hair as he licked my clit and sucked it between his lips. My back arched from the bed as his large palms pressed my thighs apart.

"I love your sweet pussy." His throaty growl had me pulling his hair.

He fastened his entire mouth to me, lashing my clit with the tip of his tongue until I was writhing and squeezing him between my thighs. He reached around my legs and gripped my breasts, pinching my nipples between his thumbs and forefingers.

"Michael!" I dug my heels into his back.

He seized my clit again, sucking and nipping at it before settling in and licking it furiously, the hard ball of his tongue piercing heightening every stroke. My pussy tightened, and he squeezed my nipples harder as I came to the edge of my orgasm. I rocked up to his mouth and looked down to him. He watched me, taking in every movement, every sigh, and his eyes sent me plummeting over the edge.

My hips froze as pleasure exploded through every nerve ending. I came on his name, over and over again, his name and nothing else. He was all I could think, all I could feel. He groaned into me as I relaxed and let my thighs fall open. He was still licking me, even though I made a half-hearted attempt to pull him away from my so-sensitive spot. He gave me one more long lick and prowled up my body.

His cock dangled hard and ready beneath him. He claimed my mouth and plunged inside me at the same time. I moaned and wrapped my arms around his neck. This was my favorite way to wake up. His tongue plundered me, rubbing against mine as he slanted over me. I was completely open to him, everything his to take and enjoy.

He started a hard rhythm and before long his hands made their way to my hair. I raked my nails down his back as he wrenched my head sideways and bit my neck. His thighs slapped into mine as he grew even rougher, just the way I wanted it.

"You like that?" He grunted, starting the dirty talk early. "My perfect little slut."

"Yes," I cooed as he pulled my hair even harder and kissed to my collarbone.

"My little whore likes getting fucked hard whenever and wherever I want. Isn't that right?" He bit my hard nipple and I shuddered.

"Yes." I gasped as he rolled my nipple between his teeth.

He moved to the other nipple, biting it even harder as I moaned and scratched his shoulders, each one of his hard strokes sending a buzz through my clit.

"That's it." He kissed up to my mouth again and braced one hand on the bed next to my head while using the other one to spread my leg out as wide as it could go. He pushed my thigh down, opening me up so I felt each impact as deeply as possible.

I closed my eyes, awash in the sensation of being filled, being surrounded by his scent, his body.

"Watch me, Jess. I want to see those gorgeous eyes when you come."

I opened my eyes and stared up into his. He was rubbing me just right, his hard chest pressing into my breasts as his cock plunged again and again. My pussy began to grip him tighter and I clutched at his back, hanging on as he brought me to the edge again.

"Come on my cock. Come for me, wildcat." His voice was guttural, strained.

I arched up to him, getting every single bit of contact on my clit. A few more hard thrusts and then I exploded in a surge of pure bliss.

He stared into my eyes as my orgasm rolled over me, delicious waves licking me as he pumped harder, pistoning into me. I wanted to close my eyes, but I couldn't. I wanted him to see what he did to me, how much he made me feel every single second of ecstasy.

"Fuck, you are so beautiful when you come." His cock grew even harder and he took my mouth again, biting my lower lip as he exploded inside me with a groan. He pumped a few more times, his cock kicking as he released. When he was finished, he eased his bite on my lip, kissing the sting away.

He sank onto me with a whoosh and wrapped his arms around me before flipping to his back, carrying me with him so I lay against his hard chest. We lay like that, him still inside me, coming down from the high and catching our breaths.

"I'm going to need a shower." Despite my words, I snuggled against him, laying my head over the ink above his heart.

"You took one last night." He kissed the crown of my head.

"Yeah, but sex hair only looks good on you, babe. Not me."

He reached down and palmed my ass, giving me a good squeeze. "Everything and nothing looks good on you, wildcat."

I smiled and nipped at his chest. "You know I love it when you call me that."

"I know you love it when I call you all sorts of things." He surged up, his cock trying to come back to life inside me.

"No, no, no." I tried to push away from him. "You are not making me late for work again."

He laughed, a deep rumble against me, and gripped my ass harder. "You aren't going anywhere, wildcat."

I pushed harder, knowing full well putting up a fight would seal my fate.

Just as I suspected, he grinned and rolled me over. I tried to shove him off and scoot away, but he didn't let me escape, didn't even let me get far enough away for his cock to slide out. Instead, he gripped my wrists and pinned them over my head.

"You know I like it when you struggle, wildcat." He grew even harder inside me.

"I can't be late for the associate meeting again. Mr. Avery will notice. And I don't want to risk losing the Frost assignment." I couldn't help moving my hips against him. But only just a little. "Especially since I'm taking so much time off for our wedding in a *week*." I tried a chiding tone, but my hips were still working at cross purposes, rubbing my clit against him.

"I can be quick." He pushed deeper into me as I shoved against his chest.

I bit my lip, my desire for him at war with my responsibilities. "No, I have to shower."

"Shower, huh?" He grinned wickedly and wrapped his arms around me before getting to his knees and walking me off the bed, all the while still inside me.

"Michael—"

He kissed me, stealing my protest as he carried me to the shower and turned the knobs. Once the water was hot, he took me inside and pinned me against the cold gray tile as the water poured over us from several different angles. He relinquished my lips and kissed down my neck, still surging inside me as I wrapped my legs tightly around him. I thought I was sated, that he couldn't wring another burst of pleasure from me, but the building pressure between my thighs said differently.

"And you say I don't know how to multitask." He laughed against my skin and bent his head to my nipple, taking it in his mouth and nipping at it.

He pushed in and out slowly now and reached down to my clit.

I moaned as he pressed his thumb against it and tried to push my hips away from him and back into the wall.

"Too much, wildcat?" He stood straight and stared into my eyes.

"Yes."

He quirked a smile and kept rubbing my clit. "Too bad."

I dug my nails into his shoulders as he picked up his pace and moved one hand to my ass, fucking me harder as our bodies slapped together, the water splashing and warming the goose bumps along my skin. He pinned me with his gaze, forcing me to watch him as he fucked me against the wall. I couldn't look away from him, didn't want to.

I relaxed my legs so he could go even deeper, fully opening to him as I submitted to his touch.

"That's it wildcat." He sped his pace on my clit, making my pussy constrict even tighter around his thick cock.

I leaned my head back against the wall and he put his forehead to mine, keeping his cock deep and pumping in shorter strokes. His chest pressed into me, my nipples sliding against his slick skin and making my body buzz with anticipation.

"Michael, please. I'm so close."

He groaned. "Going to come on my cock again?"

"Please." My stomach clenched, my hips stilling as the orgasm crested.

Right when I started to moan and my pussy clamped down on him, he grunted and pushed deep inside. His eyes bored into mine as we came together.

"Michael, Michael," I said his name on repeat as my pleasure washed over me.

He slowed his thrusts and stopped before giving me a long, wet kiss.

Pulling away, he put me on my feet – though my knees wobbled – and grabbed a loofa and my body wash.

He waggled his eyebrows. "Turn around. I want to clean you up real nice for work."

I cocked my head to the side. "Come again?"

"You heard me." He soaped up the loofah as I dutifully turned around.

He slapped my ass hard and scrubbed the loofah over my shoulders and down my back. The soapy warmth, especially when delivered by Michael, felt wonderful.

I looked over my shoulder at him. "Go easy on me. You've already worn me out for the day and it isn't even eight o'clock yet."

He laughed, the sound low and raspy. "Is that so?"

He leaned in and bit my ear, his warm breath sending shivers down my spine as he slid the loofah to my ass. "Bend over and I'll really give you something to complain about."

CHAPTER THREE
MICHAEL

"MOVE A BIT MORE to the right."

Sadie, nude save for some expertly-applied body paint made to look like a bikini, shifted as instructed and gave her best face to the camera. I took a few more shots, the southern California sun illuminating her skin and giving her a glow.

Her blonde hair flowed in beachy waves over her shoulders as she reclined against the warm sand. I was almost finished with the shoot, but I had to get her photos just right. She wanted to make the cover of the sports magazine this year, having been narrowly beaten by a bustier model the prior year.

"Sit forward a bit and turn your chest toward me. Let's make the most of the light there."

"Whatever it takes." She leaned toward me, her breasts on full display under the paint, the nipples straining to the sky. I moved toward her left, setting up a slightly different shot that highlighted every curve. My assistant moved with me, reflecting the light with a large, silver oval.

She plastered her practiced look of seduction on her face.

"Sadie, I need more from you." I lowered the camera. "I need you to imagine you're looking at your lover. A handsome man. The one who will give you everything you ever wanted. And he is about to fuck you, and you desperately want him to. Can you give me that look?"

She smiled, her teeth white and perfect. "I think I can manage."

Her expression changed, softened, but her eyes remained sharp, focused. It was just what I wanted. I snapped a few more shots, moving around her as her gaze followed me. A few more clicks and we were done.

I stepped back and scrolled through the photos on my screen. I would have put money on one of the shots in the last set; it would make the cover.

"All right, Sadie. We're done here. Go ahead and get dressed." I smiled and gave her a small salute as another assistant hurried to her with a towel.

Turning, I walked to the makeshift tent we'd set up along the shore. Once in the shade, I transferred the images from my camera to my laptop. Some of the images had promise, but I wanted to get to the last set. *Yes.* Her expression was perfect, an enticing smile to match the rest of her. The very last photo was the right one, the light giving her an effervescence that translated perfectly through my lens.

"Anything noteworthy?" The magazine editor sat beneath the tent, filling his face with random bits of food from the craft table.

"I think you'll find some keepers in here." I saved the best shots to my hard drive for editing later in my office at home. I loved working with Jess in my lap or peeking over my shoulder. She always had great input on my photos.

"So, we're done?" The editor asked and brushed coffee cake crumbs from his shirt.

I closed my laptop. "Yes. I'll have the best shots to you tomorrow."

"Good. You coming to Rio next week for that shoot?"

He stood, his portly belly bulging over his belt. He was over fifty, but flirted with the models like he was my age.

Forcing a smile, I said, "Sorry. I can't. I'm getting married in two days, then off to our honeymoon in Thailand."

He coughed and shook his head. "Why would a young man like you be taking the plunge when you're constantly surrounded with the choicest pussy?"

I stopped packing my camera and stared at him. "My personal life is none of your business, but I can assure you Jess is the best thing that's ever happened to me. I'm lucky to have her."

He ran a hand through his thinning hair and looked at me over his sunglasses. "Son, here's a bit of advice. There is nothing in this world better than strange, and model strange?" He eyed Layla, one of the models, as she cut across the sand next to the tent and lowered his voice. "That's the best of all. Don't go fucking it up by getting married."

"Thanks for the input." My hands fisted but I forced my fingers to relax before grabbing my laptop bag and camera. Showing him my revulsion wasn't an option, especially since I wanted to get more work from the magazine. "I'll be in touch tomorrow."

"Okay then." He grinned. "Think about what I said."

I walked away, out of the shade from the tent and into the sun. "Will do," I called behind me.

The sand was warm on my bare feet. It would have been a nice day at the beach if I'd spent it with Jess. Instead, I was beat and ready to get home to her. I checked my watch. She'd be done at her job in half an hour unless her crusty boss made her work late. Maybe I could make her dinner. I smiled just thinking of how surprised she'd be at a home cooked meal.

"Michael?"

I looked over my shoulder. Sadie was running through the sand to catch up. I slowed and glanced behind her where the editor stood, grinning at me from beneath the tent. Sadie wore a tiny pair of shorts and a white tank top, her nipples still as hard as they were when I was taking her picture.

"What is it, Sadie?"

"Oh, I just um, I just wanted to say thanks for the shoot." She walked to my elbow and we trudged together toward the parking lot along the scenic drive.

"Sure."

"Any of them seem like contenders?" She hooked her arm through mine.

I stopped. "Sadie."

"What?" She lowered her sunglasses and flashed her light amber eyes.

I disentangled my arm from hers. "Sadie, you know I've got a girl."

She pouted and stared at the ground. "I know you do. I just wondered if you think any of my photos were good."

"Oh." I pulled the laptop bag strap higher on my shoulder. "I think several were, actually. One from that last set has a lot of promise."

"For the cover?" She looked up at me.

"Yeah, I think for the cover."

She squealed and launched herself at me. I caught her in my arms as she pressed a big kiss to my cheek. "Thanks, Michael! You're the best."

She dropped to the ground and hurried away to her car. I laughed and followed, slipping my sandals on before following her into the gravel parking lot. Sadie waved as she reversed in her little sports car and got on the road, headed back to the city.

I dropped my equipment in my passenger seat and knocked the rest of the sand from my legs and feet. A burst of movement to my right caught my attention. The familiar flash of sun on a lens told me what was going on. The paparazzi were here.

"So, Michael, you and Sadie together now?" The

paparazzo yelled from what he likely considered was a "safe" distance. I wanted to wring his neck. How long had he been spying?

"Get bent, motherfucker." I flipped him off and took a few menacing steps toward his car. He dropped inside in a hurry, slamming his door.

I snatched up a rock from the lot and tossed it at him. It pinged off the roof of his car as he backed up and sped out onto the highway in a swirl of dust and screeching tires. I wanted to drag him out and crush his camera under my heel, but I couldn't. Even though I'd changed my ways and hadn't done anything interesting in years, the paparazzi still shadowed me, especially when I was spending the day with models. And now, thanks to Sadie's exuberance, they had some ammunition. *Fuck.*

Stalking to my car, I sank into the driver seat and pounded the steering wheel with my palm. Of all the days for this sort of a fuck up. Just forty-eight hours before our wedding, I would have to explain to Jess that I wasn't fucking a model.

CHAPTER FOUR
JESS

I HURRIED DOWN THE hallway. It was already long past five, but the partner I worked for was staying late and expected me to do the same. I'd wanted to leave early and do something special for Michael, especially with all the hectic wedding planning we'd been doing lately, but it wasn't going to happen. Mr. Avery had exacting standards, and I needed to meet them if I had any chance of a future at his law firm.

The office was empty for the day, most of the staff having already left right at five and the overworked associates leaving soon after. I hoped I wouldn't have to stay too much later.

The click clack of my heels echoed down the marble hall as I made my way past the cubicles and offices toward the corner where Mr. Avery was located. His dark wooden door was shut, so I knocked.

"Jess?" he called.

"Yes sir."

"Come in."

I opened the door and crossed the short distance to his mahogany desk. His office was mostly windows, looking out onto the city from the thirty-third floor. He was one of the firm's founders, and I was lucky he'd hired me straight out of law school.

"I have all the pleadings you asked for, including their discovery responses from March of last year." I placed the neat stack of pages on the corner of his well-organized desk.

He leaned back in his plush leather chair. "Have a seat, Jess."

Shit. At this rate, I'd barely get to see Michael at all and the next day would be filled with tons of pre-wedding preparation. I did as instructed and sank onto his leather couch, but perched on the edge. Maybe he would notice my anxiousness and let me go for the evening.

Mr. Avery was a fit fifty, attractive with only light graying in his dark hair. He wore a dark gray suit and a tie, always impeccably dressed.

"Jess, as you know, I'll need someone to help me cover the depositions in the Frost case next month."

I couldn't stop my smile. The Frost case concerned an electrical infrastructure project that had gone bad based on improper voltage specifications. Seemed boring, but the case—and all the witnesses—was located on the island of Maui. I had never dreamt of getting such a plum assignment so early in my career, though I'd daydreamed about it with Michael. He'd assured me that if I got a chance to go, he'd come along with me and show me the sights. He'd been to Maui several times for shoots.

"So, is that something you'd be interested in?" He stood and walked around his desk before sitting beside me on the sofa.

"Yes!" I exclaimed before calming my tone. "I mean, yes, Mr. Avery. I'd love that."

"I would need you to be available at all hours. The contract workers with the most information about the project problems work all sorts of different shifts. We'll have to take testimony on their time. So it's a twenty-four hour job while we're out there. Can you handle that?"

"I can do that." I tucked a lock of my dark brown hair behind my ear. "I'm so excited."

"I'm glad. You've been an exceptional associate so far." He smiled, something he rarely did.

I didn't think I could grin any bigger, but I did. He rarely praised anyone. "Thank you, sir."

"And I hope that on this trip." He put his hand on my knee, meeting the bare skin beneath the hem of my black skirt. "We can get to know each other even better."

My grin faded and my cheeks heated with something other than excitement. *Oh, god.* "Mr. Avery, I don't think you mean—"

"I know exactly what I mean." His grip tightened on my leg. "You're exceptional. We'll be spending a couple of weeks in the most beautiful spot on the planet. When I said I needed you at all hours, Jess, I meant it."

I batted his hand off my leg and rose, my heart racing. "I think we've had a misunderstanding." Disappointment warred with anger inside me, and I couldn't look him in the eye.

He stood. "Come now, Jess. Walking around here in those short skirts, batting your eyelashes at me—I haven't been imagining these things have I?"

"I-I'm afraid you have. I'm getting married in two days to the man I love." I finally met his eye. "I have no interest in you other than professionally speaking."

He frowned and stepped closer. My gorge rose but I swallowed hard.

"That's a shame. I suppose I'll have to give the Frost case to Emilia." He placed his finger under my chin. "Unless you'll reconsider your position?"

My skin crawled. "No, I won't. I'm not here to be your mistress or to fuck my way up the ladder." Anger rose inside me and spilled into my words. "Don't give me the assignment. I don't want it with its *extra duties.*" I was burning my bridge with this firm, possibly getting myself blackballed, but I would never agree to what he was suggesting.

Before I had a chance to back away, he kissed me. I shoved at his chest but he wrapped his arms around me, pressing me against him. He tried to stick his tongue in my mouth, but when I tried to bite him, he let me go.

"Jess?"

I whirled. Michael stood in the doorway behind me, an inscrutable look on his face.

Fuck.

"Michael. It's not what it looks like." This was bad. Why would I say the thing that the guilty party always says?

Michael strode into the room, his presence filling the room to bursting with what I realized was rage. Mr. Avery cleared his throat.

"Really? Because what it looks like to me is a dirty old man threatening a young female associate to try and get her to sleep with him. Sound accurate?" He held his hand out to me.

I ran to him and took it. He pulled me around behind him and placed a hand on my hip.

"That's actually … Perfectly accurate." I whispered as relief coursed through me. He squeezed my hip.

I stood on my tiptoes and peeked over Michael's shoulder. His tattoos swirled out of the neckline of his shirt, the ink seemingly alive as his veins pumped double time underneath.

He was like a furnace ready to blow.

"She has come onto me time and time again." Mr. Avery's voice quavered. "I was simply informing her that I wasn't the sort of man to cheat on my wife with an associate. That's all this was."

"You're going to lie about my girl to my face?" Michael dropped his hand from my hip and advanced on Mr. Avery.

Mr. Avery stumbled backwards and landed heavily on his couch. Michael kept walking until he loomed over the other man.

"Michael, don't hurt him." I had never seen him so angry, every muscle in his body drawn so tight he practically vibrated with malice.

He stopped and stretched his fingers before balling them into fists. Mr. Avery cowered beneath him.

"If you ever treat Jess like anything less than a lawyer deserving of respect, I'll come back here. Understand? For that matter, if I hear you've treated *any* associate the way you've treated my girl, I'll be back." He leaned down and stabbed his index finger in Mr. Avery's face. "I asked you a question."

"Y-yes, I understand." Mr. Avery squeaked.

"Now, apologize to Jess." Michael straightened and crossed his arms over his broad chest. "I'll wait."

Mr. Avery glanced to me and then dropped his gaze to the floor. "I'm sorry, Jess."

"Good. Jess won't be working for you any more, but I expect a stellar recommendation letter. If I hear any different, I'll give you three guesses of what will happen." Michael bored into Mr. Avery with his eyes. "Go on, guess."

"You'll be back." The quaver in his voice had turned into a shudder. I wondered if he might piss himself. Mr. Avery likely wasn't used to large, tattooed, pierced men with fauxhawks threatening him over his dirty deeds.

"That's right." Michael slapped Mr. Avery on the shoulder. The man jumped and paled. "You're a quick study, *Mr. Avery.*"

Michael turned back to me, not giving another glance to my ghostly white boss.

"Come on. Let's get your stuff and get the hell out of here." He took my hand. It was only then I realized I'd been shaking. Was it with anger or fear? I couldn't tell.

He pulled me into the hallway and stopped. "Which way to your office?"

He'd never visited me at work before, no matter how

many times I'd begged him to come see me. He was too worried the stuffy attorneys would judge his appearance and hold it against me. Why had he chanced it tonight?

He ran his hand down my cheek, the concern in his eyes making me melt for him like I did on the first day we met. "You okay?"

"Now that you're here, yes." I placed my hand against his chest, feeling the rapid beat of his heart. "Thank you for not hurting him."

He smirked and kissed my forehead. "He's lucky you said something or I would be committing a felony right now."

"Come on." I pulled him down the hall, away from Mr. Avery. I didn't want to risk any more run-ins.

It didn't take long to pack my few personal items. I hated giving up my job, especially when it was Mr. Avery's fault, but I couldn't stay here. I knew that much. Michael tucked my framed diplomas under his arm and I carried a small box of my belongings. I stood in the doorway for a few seconds, saying goodbye to my closet-sized, windowless office.

Michael wrapped his arm around my waist. "I'm sorry this happened. It's not fair."

"It's okay." I blinked back my tears. There were other jobs, ones that didn't come with a dickhead for a boss. I leaned against him.

"It's not, but it will be. I promise. You're a catch for any firm in this town. You'll have another job in no time."

"You always say the right thing." I smiled up at him. "You do the right thing, too."

He tensed for a moment, then led me down the corridor toward the elevators.

"Let's get home. Put this shit behind us. We have a wedding, a honeymoon, and a staggering amount of sex in our imminent future."

I laughed as we walked into the elevator. "I love you."

He leaned down and kissed my neck beneath my ear,

sending goose bumps down my body. "I love you, too."

CHAPTER FIVE
Michael

I HELD HER CLOSE, breathing in her scent after I'd sated her that night. I needed to tell her about what happened with Sadie, but she was so shaken up about the shit her boss pulled that I didn't want to make it any worse.

I nuzzled into her hair, wanting her to feel how much she meant to me, how much I loved her. She had saved me. The moment I'd seen her deep blue eyes I knew I had to turn my life around, to strive to be good enough to earn her trust.

I smiled remembering the first time we'd been together, when I'd taken her virginity. She'd been so shy, but I knew my wildcat was in there somewhere. I pulled her to my chest and she sighed, the sound of an angel.

I smoothed my palms up and down her back as she breathed deeply. I couldn't wait to make her my wife. Not to mention the fireworks I had planned for our honeymoon. I dropped one more kiss into her fragrant hair and drifted off to sleep.

***

Giggles erupted in the living room. I woke to the morning sun streaming through the windows of the penthouse I shared with Jess. She was gone, the bed cold next to me. I hated waking up without her.

"Now, girls, calm down. We have to be at the spa in fifteen minutes." My mother's voice rang out, authoritative but also tinged with the sort of joy I hadn't heard from her in a while.

"Jess, you ready?" One of her friends asked.

"Yeah, let me kiss Michael goodbye."

More laughter rang out as Jess re-entered our bedroom. She radiated happiness, all the problems of the previous day erased from her beautiful face. My cock hardened as I watched how she moved. She wore a demure white dress with some medium white heels. Something about the propriety of the dress made me want to rip it off her. I wouldn't, but I'd get at least a taste.

"Close the door," I said.

She shook her head and grabbed her bag from the dresser. "Michael, your mom is in the living room. I have to go."

"I don't give a fuck if the Pope is in the living room. Close the door, wildcat." I eased my hand under the sheet and fisted my cock, pumping it slowly as I watched her. I tossed the sheet off with my other hand and her eyes widened as she saw what I was doing. She dropped her bag and closed the door.

"Come here." I moved to the edge of the bed.

She walked over, her hips swaying in her heels. "Michael, the girls—"

"On your knees."

She stood in front of me, her hands on her hips but her eyes glued to my cock. She licked her lips. "I can't do this. Not with your mom here."

I gripped her wrists and yanked her down. She yelped as her knees hit the floor.

"Everything okay?" Jess' Aunt Carrie called.

"Fine." Jess and I said in unison.

She lowered her voice and looked up at me, her big blue eyes luminous. "You're a very bad man, Mr. Williams." Running her hands up my thighs, she licked the head of my cock.

My hips thrusted up at the contact. Her mouth, all of her, was electric. She took me to the back of her throat in one smooth movement.

"Fucking hell, wildcat. And *I'm* the bad one?"

She dug her nails into my thighs and criss-crossed her tongue along the bottom of my shaft. Then she got to work, bobbing on my cock with slippery sounds. Her tongue was velvet on me and I stifled a groan as my cock stiffened even more from her attentions.

I put a hand in her hair, but she knocked it away.

She slid me out of her mouth. "I have to look presentable when I open that door."

I growled and pulled her up, putting her on my lap so she straddled me.

She placed her hands on my chest, her fingernails digging into her own name inked over my heart.

"Be my good little slut and let me fuck that tight pussy."

"Michael," she gasped.

I claimed her mouth, her breath sweet with orange juice, and ran my hands up her skirt. She was wearing some sort of lacy panties. I gripped the sides and tugged, ripping them off her and slinging them to the floor, before palming her pussy. She moaned as I stroked down her wet flesh, my fingers teasing her clit.

My cock twitched, desperate to feel every inch of her slick wetness. I sank two fingers inside her tight pussy before withdrawing them and putting them in her mouth. She licked my fingers clean as I used my other hand to position my tip at her entrance. One thrust and I was deep inside her, bliss coating my cock as I lay back.

"Ride me, wildcat. Get off on my cock. I want to see you." I laced my hands behind my head as she began working up and down on my shaft. She was invested in her own pleasure now. I could tell from the way her lids were at half mast.

"Bad man," she panted and spread her legs wider, getting every bit of friction.

"Lift your skirt. Show me that pretty pussy. I want to see you touch yourself."

She threw her head back, exhaling to the ceiling and giving herself over to me, to us. She pulled up her skirt with one hand and teased at her clit with the other. I groaned as she rose and fell while I pumped into her, my cock demanding more and more of her.

Fuck, she was so beautiful. Her dark hair cascaded down her shoulders and her tits bounced under the white dress with each impact. I resisted the urge to grip the front of the material and rip it in two ... barely.

"I'm close." She met my eyes.

I smirked. She was in a hurry. I'd let her have it quickly, but only because we had guests. I loved taking my time with her, drawing out her orgasm for as long as possible.

Moving my hands to her hips, I forced her into a faster rhythm. I gripped the hand at her pussy and brought it to my lips, licking her honey from them as she moaned. Then I put her hand back, keeping my fingers on top of hers as she swirled and rubbed her hard nub.

My load crept up my shaft as her movements grew more erratic. Her hips bucked, her pussy spasming.

A knock at the door and then my mother's voice. "Jess, dear, we have to get going."

"I'm coming!" Jess cried as her hips froze and her pussy clamped down on me.

"Okay." A loud cough. "I'll, ah, I'll take the girls downstairs and wait for you in the limo."

I bit back my yell as I shot inside Jess, coating her pussy with me as we stared into each other's eyes. Her brow was pinched and she bit her lip to try and stay quiet. I slammed her hips down onto me, keeping her still as I emptied out my last bit of spend deep into her.

"Fuck me," she whispered and rolled off me, lying on her back and panting.

I flinched when her heat was gone, and I wanted to climb on top of her and go again. Especially since I knew this was my last chance to have her before the wedding. She was staying with her aunt tonight to get ready and keep with tradition of the groom not seeing the bride.

I rolled over on my side and raised up on my elbow, drinking in her reclining form. Gorgeous, curvy woman. I still couldn't believe she'd agreed to be mine.

"I can't believe we did that. Your mom!" She cringed.

I laughed. "She'll get over it. Besides, you were telling the truth. You were definitely coming."

She slapped at my arm. "Bad man."

"Your bad man." I kissed her, gently now.

She wrapped her arms around my neck and returned the kiss, pressing her breasts into my chest. I clutched her waist.

She broke the kiss and scooted away.

"I have to go." She tried for a sterner tone as I pulled her back to me. "No sir. Not again."

I dropped one more kiss on her swollen lips. "Fine. If you must."

"Yes." She sat up and stood, as if that would keep her from me. I could sling her back onto the bed and have her moaning again in seconds.

Instead, I lay back and watched her walk to the bathroom. She cleaned up and donned a new set of panties before heading back to the bedroom door.

I went to her, giving her another long kiss. "Next time I see you, shit's gonna get real, wildcat."

She gave me a radiant smile that made my heart warm. "I know, and then you're mine."

I placed her delicate hand over my heart. "I'm already

yours. Always have been, just didn't know it."

Tears sparkled in her eyes and I dropped another quick kiss on her lips before shooing her out the door. I never wanted to see her cry, even if they were tears of joy. I loved her too damn much.

I followed her to the elevator, unable to keep my hands off her even for a second. She laughed as I cupped her ass and gave it a good squeeze as the doors opened. Another peck on my lips and she was on the elevator.

"Try and behave yourself, Michael." She simpered, as if daring me to take her again. She drove me crazy.

"See you at the church, soon to be *Mrs. Williams*." I grinned as the elevator doors shut.

CHAPTER SIX
JESS

MY BRIDESMAIDS AND I spent the day at the spa. I thought it would be the most relaxing way to pregame before the wedding, though I couldn't help but wonder what Michael was doing. Even as the massage therapist expertly worked every bit of stress from my muscles, I wished Michael's hands were on me instead.

"Jess, honey?" Daisy, my best friend from law school and maid of honor stood next to me as I lay face down on the massage table. I recognized the butterfly tattoo on the top of her foot.

"Mmm?" I felt like I was floating, weightless from the hour-long massage, as the soothing music played low in the background.

"We have to get going. We have more appointments." She tapped her foot.

"What more appointments?" My voice was muffled by the massage table. "We've been here all day. I've been waxed, facialed, buffed, manicured, pedicured, massaged, and god knows what else."

"We have a little something fun planned for tonight." She giggled.

I craned my neck around so I could look up at her. She was tall with long blonde hair and deep brown eyes, and currently naked.

I rolled my eyes. "There are robes, Daisy. How about you try one?"

She put her hands on her hips. "If you got it, flaunt it."

"Whatever." I arched an eyebrow. "What *fun* are you talking about?" I'd specified over and over that I wanted no crazy bachelorette party. But Daisy was something of a wild card—one of the main reasons we'd become fast friends in law school.

"You'll see. Come on. Let's go." She pranced out of the room.

I groaned and sat up. Wedding planning had taken a toll on me, but the massage had gone a long way to ease my tension. Well, the massage and my time with Michael earlier in the day. Just remembering the way he watched me ride him had my cheeks warming.

Dressing in my street clothes, I slipped on my sandals and left the soothing room. My bridesmaids were lined up outside, with Daisy at the head of the procession.

"Let's hit the road, get some real food—not cucumber water—and see what else we have in store for our favorite bride to be." Daisy grinned and took off at a brisk march, the other girls following.

"Really?" I grumbled under my breath but followed all the same.

Evelyn and Aunt Carrie waited in the lobby area, laughing at the parade of girls heading out to the limo.

Evelyn gave me a hug that took my breath away. "You have fun tonight. Last night of freedom and all. Though I know for a fact my son can't wait to make an honest woman out of you."

Aunt Carrie was next, giving me an even bigger hug than I thought possible. "I'm so proud of you."

I beamed, though tears began to swim in my vision.

"Your mom is, well she'll always be your mom, but I

want you to know Evelyn and I are here for you. I can't imagine how hard it is for you right now with your mom being…"

"Uninterested in everything I do?" I filled in. My mom only had one consideration in her mind. Herself. I'd known this since I was a child. I used to hold it against her, but after a while, I only felt sorry for her. Aunt Carrie was my father's sister. He'd passed when I was very young, and Aunt Carrie had become my main cheerleader, encouraging me all the way through college and law school.

"I'm sorry." Aunt Carrie frowned. "I didn't mean to bring up bad juju. I just want you to know we're here for you. Whatever you need."

I hugged her and Evelyn again. "No bad juju. Only happy times. You are my family. Just like Michael is my family."

"I'm so glad to hear you say that, sugar." Evelyn kissed me on the cheek.

Daisy opened the front door of the spa. "Come on, *bride*, we need to hit the road."

"Love you." I squeezed Evelyn's and Aunt Carrie's hands. "I'll see you in the morning."

I followed Daisy out into the mild air as Evelyn and Aunt Carrie hugged it out with each other. They were so cute.

"Now that we're rid of the chaperones, it's time for the real fun." Daisy shoved me police-style into the back of the limo.

I laughed and joked with my bridesmaids as we drove into the heart of the city. After an over the top meal at a restaurant we couldn't have afforded without Michael's AmEx, the girls hustled me back into the limo and blindfolded me. The smooth fabric against my eyelids blocked out everything but the smallest sliver of light along the bottom.

"Start the party!" Daisy cranked up the music, the bass

thumping in my chest and I heard the sound of corks popping.

Before long a glass was shoved into my hand.

"Drink, bitch." The girls clinked their glasses with mine. When I tried to sip it, someone lifted my glass up so I drained it all in one go.

"Another for the bride." Someone steadied my hand as my glass grew heavier and again I drank it all down.

I reached to try and peel my blindfold off.

"No!" Daisy smacked my hand. "Here, I got you a crown, too. Bend over."

Someone snorted. "She'll be hearing that a lot for the next week."

Howls of laughter filled the limo and I couldn't help but smile. These were my girls, as rowdy and silly as they were. We drank and acted fools the rest of the way to wherever we were going. The limo slowed to a halt and someone opened the door to my right.

The car began rocking as my bridesmaids exited. Then someone took my hand and pulled me out.

"The sash!" Someone said.

"Right. I've got it." Daisy draped something over me and then took my hand again. All I could hear was my girls, traffic sounds, and music with another deep beat.

"Stairs, whore." Daisy giggled and led me up about five steps. We almost tripped twice, the champagne buzzing around my head. "Okay. Walk straight ahead."

The atmosphere changed from open and breezy to close and loud as we entered what I assumed was a club. The silky material against my eyes gave me no clues, but the smell of alcohol and the music informed me plenty.

"We're the Daisy Raines party." She yelled over the sound of the music and the clubgoers.

"Right this way." A man's voice.

Daisy led me through the room, around several bodies. It occurred to me that most of the voices were female.

"And here we are. Front and center. Enjoy the show."

The man's voice receded on the last words.

Daisy pushed me down into a seat and whipped the blindfold off my face. My eyes adjusted quickly in the gloom.

"This is a strip club." I turned to her. "A male strip club!" We sat in the front row along the edge of the stage. She was grinning huge, right along with my other bridesmaids.

I tried to get angry with them. I truly did. But the champagne and the glee on their faces tempered my irritation. "I said no strip clubs, Daisy."

"Just this one time. You'll love it. Live a little before you tie the knot."

I frowned.

She bumped her shoulder against mine. "Look at these girls, your dutiful bridesmaids. Don't they deserve a night of fun? After all the bridesmaid drudgery. All the dresses they tried on. The dresses they bought. The planning. The rehearsal dinner. Don't they get one night of living it up?"

"This is why you aced law school. Turning shit around on people." I raised an eyebrow but nodded. "Fine. I will allow this debauch, though I don't know how Michael's going to feel about it."

"Pfft. What Michael doesn't know won't hurt him." The girls agreed with Daisy, taking their seats and chattering about the show.

"Hi. I'm Trey. I'll be your server this evening." A young man, dressed in only a tight pair of black bikini bottoms appeared with a bottle.

Daisy stood and tucked a twenty into his briefs, getting a look down the front as she did so. "Well, Trey, we're the party and this is our bachelorette, so treat us right."

Trey glanced down to me and smiled. "Cum dumpster?"

I tilted my head. Had I heard him correctly? "What?"

He was staring at my chest. I looked down and saw that the sash Daisy had put on me said "cum dumpster."

"Daisy!" I tried to pull it off.

"No, no. It's great actually." Trey laughed as he poured us all another round of champagne. "The guys are going to love it."

I fumbled with the sash. "The guys are goin—"

The music cut off my protests and the lights came up to glaringly bright before settling back down.

A man strolled onto the stage, dressed like a dapper don. Pinstriped suit, slick dark hair, and what I could tell was a killer body underneath. "Welcome, ladies. I'll be your host for the evening. My name's Big Stick."

A host of catcalls, including Daisy's, went up from the crowd.

"We have a special bachelorette party here tonight. I believe a young lady named Jess is the lucky bride to be?" He scanned the front row and seized on me, the crown and sash giving me away. He pointed at me. "Tonight is your night, little girl."

The lights dimmed and Daisy tilted my glass again, making me drink so fast I almost choked.

A familiar song started to play, but the beat hadn't dropped yet. The lights came up and three men were onstage. Big Stick was out front, and they were all dressed similarly – suits, ties, and hats. They were still, waiting. The crowd was still, too, waiting right along with the performers. High notes came to a crescendo as the crowd practically salivated in silence.

When the beat finally dropped, the men began to move and all hell broke loose in the club. Women screamed and tossed bills onto the stage as the men danced in perfect suggestive unison. Daisy made sure my glass remained full as we watched.

When they ripped their suits off and wore only ties and tight black briefs, Daisy jumped up and applauded. I was ensnared, watching them roll their rippling abs as they moved effortlessly around the stage. I could see the appeal, especially with how packed their shorts appeared to be.

When Big Stick hit the deck in front of us and began shadow-fucking the floor, I felt heat rising and blooming in my cheeks. When he rose and jumped down to our row, I tried to shrink back in my seat, but he walked right past the screaming Daisy and stood in front of me. Pointing, he mouthed *you*.

I shook my head. He grinned. Daisy grabbed my arm and yanked me up. Big Stick lifted me by my ass before carrying me onstage.

The words *oh shit* were on repeat in my mind as he laid me down and mimicked eating my pussy and then fucking me.

"Grab my shoulders. I won't bite." He said and ground his cock against me. "This is your show."

I gripped his slick shoulders, my fingers barely able to get any traction.

"It's all a show. Congratulations on your wedding." Big Stick smiled and then mimicked eating my pussy again before helping me to my feet and back down to my seat.

Daisy crowed with laughter. "Wasn't that the best thing ever?"

Clearly, she'd never had sex with Michael Williams. Otherwise, she'd know nothing was ever better than that. As it was, I shrugged and sat.

The girls thoroughly enjoyed the rest of the show. Thankfully, Big Stick seemed to realize I didn't enjoy the spotlight, so he used Daisy as my proxy, flipping her upside down and doing any number of sexual things to her for the crowd. I laughed and had a great time, throwing bills right along with the rest of my bridesmaids.

By the time the show was over, my head was cloudy and I wanted nothing more than to go to bed.

On our way out, Big Stick stopped me at the door and gave me a hug. "I meant what I said. Congratulations. Thanks for playing along. Give me a call if the wedding goes south."

He pressed into my hip with his palm and then pulled

away. I smiled and waved bye as Daisy helped me down the stairs. And then we were on our way out into the night. The limo dropped me off at my aunt's house.

Daisy walked me to the stoop and helped me ring the doorbell. I was having trouble getting it to stay in one place long enough for me to press it.

She helped me stand up straight, running her fingers along the sash with one hand and steadying me with the other. "I hope you had a good time. That was all I wanted, you know?"

I smiled and hugged her. "It was fabulous. And one thing's for certain, I'll never forget it."

Aunt Carrie opened the door and took one look at me before turning the evil eye on Daisy. "I thought I told you to go easy on her!"

"I did." Daisy stepped away from the door, retreating from Aunt Carrie's wrath. "Give her the cocktail I told you about and she'll be fine."

"Another cocktail?" I asked as Aunt Carrie pulled me inside.

She had rollers in her hair. She reminded me of Medusa with pink snakes on her head.

"Did you just call me Medusa?"

"Did I say that out loud?" I asked.

She wrung her hands. "Oh, Lord. You look like crazy hell. Come on in the kitchen. She slammed the door, cutting off Daisy's laughing apology.

I giggled and followed her to the kitchen. She pulled a glass from the fridge that had some sort of greenish concoction in it.

"Drink it. We can't have you hungover for your wedding." She proffered the glass.

"What's in it?"

"Doesn't matter. Drink it."

I shrugged. I'd already downed plenty of mystery drinks that night. What was one more? I took the glass and drank as much of it as I could stand before dropping the rest of it down the sink. "Yick!"

"Okay, off to bed with you." She helped me to her guest room and got me under the covers. After that, it all went black.

CHAPTER SEVEN
MICHAEL

I COULDN'T SIT STILL.

"Everything's perfect, man. Everything." Craig, my best man sat and watched me come apart.

"It's going to be a beautiful ceremony." Paul, Craig's husband, added to the chorus of "calm the fuck down" that all of my groomsmen had been singing to me.

We were crowded in a room off the main church sanctuary. It was far too hot and I wanted to rip the tie off my neck.

My groomsmen stared as I first stood, then sat, then paced. They were a mix of models, photographers, and some friends from my darker days before I met Jess. But they were all good men, to the last one.

"I have to see her." My heart was beating out of my chest. If I could just see her, just touch her, I could calm down.

"That's against tradition." Paul shook his head.

"I don't give a fuck about tradition." I went to run my hand through my hair but Paul stood and held out his hand.

"Stop! The stylist worked too hard on that perfect fauxhawk for you to fuck it up."

I dropped my hand. He was right.

"Okay, I have an idea." Paul smiled.

"Famous last words." Craig crossed his arms over his chest.

"No, babe, it'll work. Hang on. I'll be right back." Paul hurried out.

I paced even more, peeking out the clear sections in the stained glass to see the neverending procession of guests arriving. *I need you Jess.*

After far too many minutes, Paul returned and waved me out the door. "Come on."

My heart thumped against my ribs with the hope he'd thought of some way for me to see her. I followed him through the back church hallway and down a side aisle to the church lobby.

Craig was on my heels. "Is this a good idea?"

Paul whirled. "Remember how nervous I was before we got hitched?"

"Yes." Craig nodded. "You only tried to call it off a half a dozen times."

"What did it take to get me down that aisle?"

Craig grinned. "If I remember correctly, a kiss and a little something else."

"Exactly. Now, I love you, but shut the fuck up." Paul turned and kept hurrying through the church.

I was just glad that I seemed to be moving in Jess' direction. We entered the church lobby and I could almost feel Jess nearby.

"This way." Paul pressed past a couple of guests and into a side hallway. He ran right into Daisy, who'd blockaded a door that was marked "bride's quarters" on a cutesy chalkboard.

The maid of honor narrowed her eyes at me and stood up straighter, staring me down.

What the fuck is her problem?

"I just want to see her, okay?" I said. Daisy and I weren't fast friends, but I didn't know why she was looking at me like I was the enemy.

"Really?" She pulled a crumpled piece of paper from behind her back and shoved it into my hand. "You sure you don't want to see *her* instead?"

I opened the paper. I could feel the blood drain from my face as I saw the photograph. It was the one the paparazzo took of Sadie and me after the shoot at the beach. It looked even worse than I thought—her pressed against me in what looked like an intimate embrace as she kissed me. From the angle, it looked as if she were kissing me on the lips. *Motherfucker.*

I balled the paper in my fist, squeezing my fingers until it was nothing but a tiny wad of bullshit. "Has she seen this?"

"Yes," Daisy hissed and leaned toward me. It would have been menacing if she weren't built like a ballerina.

"Daisy, move." I would do whatever it took to explain the photo to Jess.

"No." Daisy put her hands on her hips.

I could have easily manhandled her out of the way, but I was in enough trouble as it was. Still, I took a step toward her, hoping to intimidate her. Nope, she just kicked her chin up and dared me to do shit about it. No wonder Jess loved her.

"Daisy, please." Craig said from over my shoulder. "You and I both know that Michael's head over heels in love with Jess. That photo doesn't mean shit. Let him by."

She pointed her finger in my face, so close it almost touched my nose. "You better have a good goddamn explanation, because if you don't, I will have your goddamn balls in a jar on my mantle. *If* I can find a small enough jar. Wait here." Daisy turned and disappeared behind the door. I couldn't catch a glimpse of what was inside, though the space looked roomier than the groom's quarters.

After a few moments, the bridesmaids filed out, their eyes downcast.

"Come in," Daisy called.

I darted in, desperate to find Jess, to explain.

"Whoa." Daisy blocked my path and held up a swatch of cloth. "Turn around. You can't see her before the wedding. I've already blindfolded her. I don't know if her seeing you is bad or not, but I'm not risking it. Once your eyes are covered, you can talk to her."

If she'd said "I'm going to drive bamboo shoots under your fingernails and then you can talk," I wouldn't have cared. I would have held my hands out and waited impatiently for her to get it done. I had to get to Jess.

I bent down and let her tie the sash.

"Okay, follow me." She led me a few steps and then directed me to sit.

A sniffle caught my ear and a piece of my heart froze and shattered. Jess was crying.

"She's sitting right next to you. I'm going to stand outside. Jess, yell if you need me."

"O-Okay." Another sniffle.

I reached my hand out next to me and patted around until I found hers. She didn't pull away at least.

"Let me explain."

"Okay. Explain why you were kissing a model."

I winced, but I wasn't going to pass up this chance. "I was doing the swimsuit edition shoot. Sadie wanted to know if she made the cover. She hugged me and kissed me *on the cheek*. That was it. I told her that you're my girl. She knows I love you. She just wanted to know if she made the cover. I swear, baby. Please don't cry. I can have my assistant get her number if you want. You can call her. I promise you're the only one for me. I love you. I would never do that to you. I swear on my life." I ended my plea on a desperate note.

I was foolish for not telling her sooner. I'd gone to her office that night to tell her, but then put it off because of what happened with Mr. Avery. And after that, I'd forgotten about it.

She took a deep, shaking breath. "I believe you."

I could breathe again. My heart beating, but only for her.

"I want to see you so bad, baby." I clutched her hand and kissed the back of it. "To look in your eyes and tell you how much I love you."

"I know. I missed you." Her voice still crackled with tears, but it was clearing up. "I knew you wouldn't. I just knew it. But I wanted to be sure."

"It's okay. I should have told you about it when it happened. I intended to, but that was the day at your office..." I didn't want to bring up that bad memory on our wedding day.

"I understand." She squeezed my hand. "And I have something to confess, too."

I tensed and tried to keep my voice calm, any number of dark ideas trying to crowd my frontal lobe. "What's that?"

"Daisy took me to an all-male review last night. Strippers." She sounded horrified.

I couldn't subdue my chuckle. "It's okay, babe. It was your bachelorette party and with Daisy, I expected nothing less."

She sighed, a relieved sound that soothed me right along with her. "Thank god. I was so embarrassed." She paused. "Wait, did you go to a strip club, too?"

I laughed again. "No. The boys offered but we stayed in and had a video game fest instead. Is that all right?"

"That's... That's actually perfect." She giggled. "Dorks."

I laced my fingers through hers. "You're the only one for me, Jess. Forever. I need you to know that."

"I do. I can't wait to be your wife."

I ran my hand up her arm, goose bumps breaking out along her bare skin. "So, now that we've made up, perhaps we can do something to seal the deal?"

"We can't see each other before the wedding." Her voice was chiding.

I grinned and dropped to my knees. "I don't need to see you to eat your pussy."

CHAPTER EIGHT
JESS

"MICHAEL, YOU CAN'T," I said, but he was already lifting up my skirt.

He ran his hands along my garters. "Oh, I like these. A lot."

Pushing my thighs apart, he exhaled along my thighs.

I squirmed and tried to close my legs. The blindfold just made the sensations stronger, every touch amplified a thousand times.

He pushed harder. "Oh no, wildcat. I need a taste. Just a quick one. The real feast comes later tonight."

His fingers inched up my thighs and then he fingered the edge of my white lace panties. "I bet these look amazing." He pushed them aside.

"Michael," I reached down to his hair.

"No." He swatted my hand away. "Do you have any idea how much trouble I'd be in if you messed up my 'do?"

I laughed but then his mouth was hot and wet against me and I gripped the sofa, digging my nails into the fabric.

"Oh my god."

He made an mmm sound against me and licked from

my entrance to my clit.

"Michael, please," I gasped. "We're in a church!"

My plea fell on deaf ears. He pressed harder against my thighs and fastened his mouth around my nub, lashing it with his tongue, the piercing touching me just right. My hips moved against him despite my efforts to resist. When he sank two fingers inside me, I was gone. I rubbed my pussy against his face, ignoring where I was, what I was wearing, the fact that I was getting married in under an hour. All I could think was how good his mouth felt on me, how amazing his fingers worked inside me.

I was fucking his face in the house of the Lord and nothing short of a lightning bolt or being dowsed with holy water would make me stop.

The pressure built inside me. He was holding nothing back, going after my clit and moving his fingers on my spot. My hips were wild against him, rubbing his face, his tongue. He groaned as I seized and made a strangled sound. I came in a rush, shattering and calling his name as he continued to tongue me beneath my wedding dress. When my body finally relaxed, he withdrew his fingers, kissed my pussy, then straightened my panties.

I could feel him standing and pushing down the stack of tulle that was my skirt.

"I don't know if this looks right, and not just because I can't see it." He kept patting the dress.

"It's fine. I'll fix it. It's—"

"Glad you lovebirds made up." Daisy's voice. How long had she been in here?

"I just walked in. Calm down. Though everyone in the church heard you moaning 'Michael' you dirty hussy." Daisy laughed.

I wanted to melt into the couch.

"Come on, Michael. Don't you have a woman to mar— Jesus, you are the most beautiful bride I've ever seen." Craig's voice.

I smiled in what I thought was his direction.

"Ok, all boys out. Go. Now." Daisy barked orders.

"I love you," I said.

Michael patted around until he found my hand again and dropped another reverent kiss on the back of it. "I love you, too, Jess. See you at the altar."

CHAPTER NINE
JESS

I TURNED OVER, LETTING the warm sun play along my back.

"All right, all right, all right." Michael did his best Matthew McConaughey impression and grabbed the bottle of sun screen. "Do you have any idea how much I love it when it's time to re-apply?"

"I think I have a pretty good idea, yes. Especially given that I haven't gotten so much as a single tan line the entire time we've been here." I laughed as he undid the clasp at the back of my bikini top and started slathering me with lotion.

"You're fair. I like your skin just like it is. Well, I like to add bite marks from time to time." He moved his hands lower, going much further than necessary into my bottoms with the sunscreen.

He'd given me plenty of bite marks during the three days we'd been in this paradise. We were honeymooning on a small island off the coast of Thailand. The sun was warm every day, the water lapping gently at the shore. It was the most beautiful place I'd ever seen.

But the nights were by far the best part. Michael and I

seemed to be on a non-step sex binge ever since the preacher pronounced us husband and wife. He'd taken me into one of the antechambers right after the ceremony and made it official before the reception. Then again after the reception. Then again once we reached our hotel that night.

I sighed as he continued rubbing the lotion down my legs. I should have felt self conscious, I supposed, given that I was curvier than the models he used to date. I wasn't. He always made me feel beautiful, no matter what I was wearing or how I thought I looked. I smiled as he lotioned each toe and giggled when he put his fingers in-between them.

"Stop! You know I can't handle that. It's tickle torture."

"Have to cover all my bases, wildcat. Any red on this gorgeous body will be coming from my hands, not the sun." Once he was satisfied that even the strongest rays weren't going to touch me, he lay back on his divan. Adjusting his sunglasses, he said, "I can't wait for you to flip over again."

Given that the last time I flipped to my back, he'd pulled down my bottoms and fucked me hard until I came screaming his name, I couldn't wait, either.

We had the entire swath of beach to ourselves. He'd planned our honeymoon to perfection. The villa where we were staying was far too large for just the two of us, but he'd wanted the best – best house, best beach, best food. I was stuffed in more ways than one every night.

I eventually dozed off to the sound of the gentle waves and woke to him standing over me.

"Let's go up, *Mrs. Williams*. Your snoring is cute, but your stomach growling means it's time to eat."

I sat up and stretched. "I don't snore."

"Sure you don't." He pulled me to my feet and we climbed the steps to the house.

Ms. Pim was already cooking when we walked through

the kitchen.

"Smells great," I said as she smiled. She was small and maybe sixty years old or so. She lived in the villa year-round and took care of all the guests. I'd grown so fond of her that I kind of wanted to kidnap her and bring her back with us to San Diego.

"Let's change and then eat and then I'd like to eat again in private." Michael scooped me up and threw me over his shoulder.

I beat at his back, but he just laughed and carried me to our bedroom on the second floor. He put me down and I scurried into the bathroom, still not quickly enough to avoid his swat on my ass.

"What do you want to wear out of the black suitcase?"

"Umm." I swiped my hair up into a high ponytail and removed my bathing suit, hanging it on the glass door to the shower. "The pink cover up, I guess." I rinsed my face with cool water.

"I have no idea what that even..." He trailed off.

"What is it?" I walked back into our room. Michael was sitting naked on the bed with a business card in his hand.

"What's that?" I pulled out a pair of panties from the suitcase and put them on, but he didn't move, just stared at the card.

I sat down next to him. "Michael? You okay?"

His green eyes met mine. "Who's Big Stick?"

"What?" The name was familiar and utterly ridiculous, but I couldn't quite place it.

"Why do you have a card with the name Big Stick and a phone number on it in your pocket?" He pointed to the white dress I'd worn to my bachelorette party. I'd just thrown it in with everything else when I'd packed up at my aunt's house before the wedding.

When I realized where I'd gotten the card, I laughed. Michael didn't.

"Who is he, Jess?" A muscle ticked in his jaw.

"A stripper." I bit his shoulder and batted my eyelashes

at him as he glowered.

"Why do you have a stripper's card in your pocket?" His voice was strained and his mouth was a thin line.

I crawled into his lap so I straddled him. "Because I think he must have slipped it in my pocket as I was leaving the club. Remember the guy I told you about that embarrassed me and took me up on stage?"

"That was Big Stick?" he asked.

"Right." I nuzzled against his neck. His jealousy turned me on more than seemed appropriate.

He gripped my ass and pulled me even closer. "Does he know you're mine?"

"Well, he did say congratulations on my wedding, but then gave me his card, so I don't know if—"

In one smooth movement, Michael ripped my panties off and tossed me onto my back. "Say you're mine."

I shrugged. "I mean, I guess you could say I'm maybe—"

He pushed inside me and I squealed at the sudden intrusion. He smoothed his cock out and then back in, as deeply as he could go.

"Now, tell me you're mine." His voice was a low growl and he bit my neck to make his point.

I gave in. I always did. There was nowhere else I'd rather be, no other man for me. "I'm yours."

"And I'm yours." He kissed me, his mouth expertly making a slave out of me as he fucked me wildly.

I lifted my hips to meet his thrusts as he clutched me to him. He grew rougher, as if trying to instill himself in every cell of my body. He was already there. Every piece of me was linked with a piece of him.

He reached between us and rubbed my clit, making me moan and writhe with each of his hard impacts. "Michael!"

"Look in my eyes. Can anyone else fuck you like this?"

I stared at him, marveling at the intensity of his gaze as he pistoned into me harder than I thought possible. Every impact jarred me and gave me so much pleasure I was panting. His thumb on my clit was working me into a frenzy.

"No," I breathed.

"Can any other man give you what you need?"

"No. Only you."

"Damn right. I'm going to come so deep inside you, wildcat. Mark my goddamn territory." He nipped at my jaw before kissing to my neck and sucking my skin between his teeth.

I dug my nails into his back and held on for the ride. My breasts pressed against his chest and I cried out as he gripped my hair, wrenched my head to the side, and bit down hard on my throat. The sting of pain intensified every sensation and I came all at once, rushing over the cliff and calling his name as I fell.

"Fuck yes, wildcat," he grunted and sank deeply inside me. His cock grew even harder and kicked as he filled me.

My pussy spasmed one final time and I shuddered beneath him. He kissed the bite on my throat before working his way to my mouth.

His lips were gentle, the frenzy gone.

"I just couldn't stand the thought of someone else touching you," he whispered against my mouth.

I wrapped my arms around his neck. "I'm yours. For as long as you want me. I'm yours. I love you."

He smiled and pulled back, wiping a sweaty lock of hair from my forehead as he stared deeply into my eyes. "Forever, then. You're mine forever."

F*ck of the Irish

CHAPTER ONE
LAUREL

"SHEEP."

I shook my head. "Try again. Ship. See? It has the short 'i' sound."

"Sheeeeeep." Wi screws her lips together, as if puckering will give her the vowel sounds she wants. It doesn't.

I had been tutoring her for months, and she'd grasped a great deal of the English language and pronunciations, but some words still escaped her. She'd been a fast learner, having come to the U.S. for college with only a rudimentary knowledge of English. Her native Chinese, though, was flawless.

I closed her workbook.

"You've almost got it. Keep practicing and I'll see you on Tuesday."

She smiled and gave me a slight nod. "Tuesday."

I leaned back in my chair, my joints stiff from sitting so long and helping her with her marine biology paper. She had a presentation coming up and didn't want to say 'sheep' when referencing the ship she was on when she took part in discovering a new species of sea mollusk.

She tucked a lock of her short dark brown hair behind her ear. "Tuesday. I will have it. Sheep."

I smiled. "Right, ship."

"Thank you, Laurel." She put great emphasis on perfecting her 'l' sounds and it showed. I was certain she would have a workable "ship" pronunciation next time I saw her.

"You are very welcome." I gathered my notebook and stuffed it into my green backpack. "Next time, then. I can find my way out. Go on. I know you want to practice."

She grinned and nodded again before hurrying out the door. We always met in a study room at the university's international house. It had become my home away from home ever since I began tutoring.

Now that my day was over, I looped my long blonde hair up into a ponytail and shrugged on my backpack. I needed to get back over to my dorm, warm up a frozen dinner, and work on my translation homework. It was only my sophomore year, but I had my heart set on grad school. Finishing a modern translation of Ovid's *Metamorphoses* from Latin to English would be my ticket into a prestigious grad school.

I walked out of the study rooms and into the main common area of the international house. Couches and bean bags were scattered around the room, students sitting and talking or typing on their laptops. I scanned the room, looking for a certain student, but Eamon was nowhere to be seen.

I sighed my disappointment and strode to the wide double doors leading into the night. Reaching for the handle, I drew back quickly as the doors swung inward.

Eamon, laughing and looking over his shoulder, barreled right into me. I made a startled squeak and lost my footing. I shot one hand out in front of me as I fell, trying to grab onto anything to stay upright. A large palm gripped my forearm and yanked me forward.

I ended up pressed against Eamon's chest, his arm

around my waist. I inhaled, taking in the scent of his aftershave—a clean, masculine smell.

"You all right?" A deep rumble against my cheek.

I pulled away from him and looked up to his eyes. They were dark blue with a mischievous sparkle. His full lip curled up in a smile, and he held my elbows as he peered down at me. He was a good foot taller than me, and I was five foot four. My heart warmed, sending a shot of pink to my cheeks as he focused on me. I dropped my gaze to the belt of his jeans, which only made me blush more.

I'd crushed on him from afar for months. But I'd never spoken to him, just listened to his lilting Irish accent and peeked at him whenever he wasn't looking. Something about him called to me, partly good looks, but also something else. He'd caught me staring every so often, each time giving me an inviting smile. On each occasion, I'd fled to my study room or left the international house altogether.

"Laurel, isn't it, love?" He put a gentle finger under my chin and lifted my face to his. "You okay?"

My lungs seemed to completely deflate. "I, um, I'm fine."

"I didn't see you there. Apologies." His lips were moving but all I could think was Eamon. His name played through my mind on repeat.

"Come on, man." Noel, one of the British students, punched Eamon in the arm. "She's fine."

Eamon barely moved. He played soccer and was ridiculously well muscled, not shirking his upper body workouts in the least.

"I know she's *fine*. I want to make sure she's okay." Eamon watched as my cheeks grew even hotter.

"I'm good." As much as I wanted his attention, wanted to lose myself in his eyes, I couldn't. "I have to go."

I side-stepped him, immediately wanting the warmth

of his touch back, and walked out into the cold night.

CHAPTER TWO
EAMON

SHE'D BEEN IN MY arms. Right where she belonged, finally. But then she'd escaped. I wanted to grab her and toss her over my shoulder, take her to my room and horse it in as rough as I pleased. But she wasn't that sort of betty. I'd learned that quite a long time before, when I'd dated her roommate.

Claudia had been a tiger in the sack, but she didn't have enough going on upstairs to keep my interest. Her major was aerobics after all. But she'd been good enough to introduce me to Laurel, and I'd been smitten ever since. I'd dropped Claudia the day I met Laurel. Needless to say, Claudia was none too pleased with me, and Laurel avoided me at all costs.

"Come on, you todger. I want to kill some terrorists in *Call of Duty.*"

"Shut your gob, you bloody cocktrough." I shoved Noel harder than I'd intended and he skittered into one of the lounging students.

"Hey!" Pablo turned around on the couch and opened his mouth to go off, but returned to his book when he got one look at my face.

"Sorry, chum. I didn't know you had a taste for that little bit of snatch." Noel shrugged and ran a hand through his dark hair.

"Don't call her that." I stalked past him and took the steps two at a time to the second floor dormitory.

Bursting through my door, I tossed my satchel on the floor and sank onto my bed. I exhaled and moved to my back, staring at the water stain on the ceiling that I'd always found looked like a bunny missing an ear.

Laurel's scent was still on my shirt. I pulled the fabric up to my nose and inhaled, as if I could ingest every small particle of her she'd left behind. My cock hardened in my pants, straining against my zipper until I had to shift.

The door opened. "Sorry, Eamon." Noel poked his head in, his blond hair lit from the hallway fluorescents.

"It's cool."

He came the rest of the way in and closed the door before sitting on his bed and flicking on a lamp. "So that's the girl I hear you talking to in your sleep?"

My eyes widened. "What?"

"Yeah." He grinned. "You say some pretty nasty shite, you filthy wanker. Very enjoyable. Something about how you're going to spank her ass raw and force her to worship your cock."

I would have felt uncomfortable if Noel hadn't brought a different betty home every night, fucking her until the wee hours before sending her packing. As it was, I flipped him off and settled back against my pillow.

"Just jump her bones and seal the deal." He pulled out his laptop and started doing some homework for once. "What's the problem?"

"Claudia."

"You think that bird still cares what you do?"

"I know she does." I pulled out my phone and scrolled to a couple of messages I'd received earlier in the day. I held it up, Noel squinted from his twin bed to read the texts.

Want to have dinner sometime? ~C
I really miss you. ~C
I wish you'd talk to me. ~C

"What the fuck, Eamon?" He shook his head and leaned back against the wood paneled wall. "Did you just give her that good of a toss in the sack?"

"I fucked her once. I really wish I hadn't." If I could have taken it back, I would have.

It had happened three months ago after I'd met her at one of the bars on the strip in our small college town. Despite my misgivings, she talked me into staying the night in her dorm room. We'd both been pretty trashed. I'd passed out and awoken to the sight of an angel standing above, looking down with a look of utter disgust.

"Laurel," Claudia had croaked, "Meet Eamon, my boyfriend."

Laurel, my angel, had pursed her perfect lips, turned her back to me, and lay on her bed, facing the wall. Though it gave me an excellent view of her choice arse, I could tell she didn't even want to look at Claudia or her "boyfriend."

From that moment, Laurel owned my heart, though all I owned was her scorn. She wouldn't give me a chance to explain, always avoiding me at the international house. And now, when I'd finally gotten a chance to touch her, to talk to her properly, she'd run like a frightened fawn.

I stared at the mangled bunny imprint on the ceiling, tracing its outline as my thoughts strayed back to how good it felt to have Laurel in my arms.

"So, I say Schrodinger's cat is dead as fucking dead can be." Noel tried to distract me.

I turned my face to the wall. "I don't want to play this stupid game."

"Dead." Noel crowed behind me. "No way it can possibly be alive."

We'd had ridiculous long-ranging arguments over Schrodinger's cat for the four years we'd been roommates at university in the States. All the arguments were dumb, circular, and usually ended in some colorful profanity. We were both training to be physicists, setting our sights on working for the American entrepreneur who'd brought back space exploration.

"That pussy perished," he said. It was admirable, really, but I didn't want to talk to him. I wanted Laurel.

"Simply no way for it to be alive." He tapped away on his keyboard.

I sighed and turned back to him. "The cat is alive and dead."

"Nope, dead."

"The cat is alive and dead until it is observed and reality collapses into the one possible outcome. You fail physics, especially quantum physics, and you will never get off the ground, much less out of Earth's atmosphere, you standing prick."

He peeked over his laptop, crinkles around his eyes from his grin. "Dead."

"Ornery cunt." But I smiled as I said it.

We batted a few more theories back and forth before settling in for the night. Though I spoke and interacted and tried to play it cool, my thoughts were constantly pulled back to Laurel. Her amber eyes and innocent smile. I'd itched to make her mine for so long that having her in my grasp made my need for her burn even higher.

I let my eyes close, forcing myself to rest for my classes in the morning and football, or as the Americans insisted on calling it "soccer," practice in the afternoon.

I was almost asleep, Laurel's eyes lulling me to slumber, when my phone pinged.

Lunch tomorrow? ~C

I groaned and tossed my phone to my desk.

"Claudia?" Noel asked, though I couldn't see him in the dark.

"Too right." Would I ever be rid of her?

"Hmm."

"Hmm what?" I asked.

"I have an idea."

I rolled my eyes. "That's the most worrying phrase I think I've ever heard you utter."

"Hear me out, wanker."

I was desperate to have Laurel. To the point I was open to any suggestions, even if they came from Noel. "What's floating around in your noggin, then?"

"Okay, here's the plan . . ."

CHAPTER THREE
LAUREL

"I CAN'T. SORRY." I shook my head lightly at Pablo.

"Maybe just coffee then?" He tried again.

"No, I don't want to get involved with anyone I'm tutoring. What if it went badly and then you didn't have anyone to work with you on papers?" Truth was I wasn't interested in Pablo, though he was a ridiculously attractive undergrad from Uruguay.

He shrugged. "Never hurts to ask."

I smiled. "True. I'll see you Wednesday. This paper is coming along nicely, but work on your transitions, okay?"

"I will. See you then." He rose and ambled out of my study room, closing the door behind him.

I breathed a sigh of relief and pulled out my translation work. With fifteen minutes before my next appointment, I could get at least a few words of my own project finished. I spent at least five minutes agonizing over the correct translation of a single word. The issue with translation from Latin was that it was a dead language, so there was no way to know exactly what feeling or resonance the particular words possessed relative to the total text. For example, the simple translation might be "blue" but a closer analysis of the text could reveal that the author actually meant "azure" or "cerulean" or something else entirely.

I stared at the letters until I had to lean back a bit just to get some context. I let out a short cry of surprise when I saw Eamon leaning against the door frame. How long had he been there? I didn't even notice the door opening.

"Hi." He smiled, dimples appearing in his cheeks. He wore a soccer jersey and jeans, his hair still wet from his after practice shower. It was embarrassing that I knew his schedule, but I was so attracted to him that it was painful. Watching him from afar was my only option, and I certainly watched every chance I got.

He ran a hand through his light brown hair. My chest warmed and the feeling spread through my stomach to the apex of my thighs. I squeezed my legs together to try and ward off the sensation.

Eamon was a player. Worse than that, my friend Claudia was head over heels in love with him. He was off limits, no matter how much I craved him.

"Hi." I wanted to look away, but couldn't. He kept me still with the weight of his gaze.

"So." He moved from the wall and sank down in the seat opposite me. "Want to go get some dinner?"

"I-I have an appointment." My voice quavered and was far breathier than it should have been.

"Mai Ling cancelled." His smile widened.

"What. How do you kno—"

"It's true. I just saw her and Pablo heading up to his room."

My stomach twirled, like a sea of butterflies were shifting and circling. "Well, in that case I should keep working on my translation." I managed to break his gaze and stared down at my notebook.

"You have to eat, Laurel."

I closed my eyes, letting his lilting accent sink into my mind. The way he said his 'l's had my heart speeding up a beat or fifty faster.

"I do, but I can eat at my dorm room."

"You're inviting me to your room?"

I glanced up to him. He still smiled, his eyes full of mischief. I caught the scent of his aftershave and my nipples hardened. He glanced down, no doubt noticing them through my t-shirt. *Oh, god.*

I pulled my jacket tighter around me and threw my notebook into my backpack. "I should go."

"Your place it is, then."

I stood and pulled my backpack on. "That's not what I meant."

"I know, but a bloke can hope, right?" He rose and took his position in the doorframe again. He wasn't threatening – though just the thought of him threatening me had my pussy heating and growing wet – only casually blocking my way.

I walked to him, facing him with a bravado I didn't feel. "I need to get back. So, if you'll excuse me…"

He didn't move as my words trailed off and I met his eyes again. They burned, our bodies too close, the heat radiating from him and into me. His scent, his skin so close.

"Let me buy you dinner." He reached out and straightened the collar on my jacket, his fingertips grazing my skin.

I closed my eyes from the softness of his touch, though I wanted it much, much rougher. I'd imagined him inside me, fucking me from behind, eating my pussy, giving it to me rough up against a wall – any possible scenario – for months. Once Claudia was asleep, I would touch myself and think about Eamon, his body mastering mine, holding me down, giving me every inch. Color burst in my cheeks and I studied my feet, worried Eamon might somehow be able to read my thoughts.

"I can't go to dinner with you."

He stroked his finger along my chin until I looked up

at him.

"Why not?" He leaned toward me, too close.

"You know why. Claudia."

"Don't worry about her." He came ever closer, our breaths mingling.

I wish I didn't have to worry about her, but she was obsessed with Eamon. Even though she'd brought home plenty of other guys since her initial hookup with him, she still went on and on about how he was the one. "She's my friend. She's in love with you."

"I don't think that's true. And I'm certainly not in love with her." His lips were only a whisper away.

I wanted to taste him, all of him. I'd only been with a few men, but something told me Eamon would erase them all out of my memory. Chill bumps broke out along my arms at the thought. Ceding ground, I stepped back, though it took every bit of willpower I had.

"She would kill me."

He tilted his head to the side. "But you want to? Go with me, I mean? You just won't because of her?"

I bit my cheek to keep from giving him the answer he wanted – the truth – that I would love to go with him. "I can't."

"What if I told you she was out on a date tonight?"

I shrugged. "She goes on plenty of dates."

"Is that so? Then how can she be in love with me?"

I'd asked the very same question plenty of times.

"Listen, all I want is dinner. Nothing else. Can you at least give me that or do I need to make a tutoring appointment?" His eyes flickered down to the desk and then back to me.

Thoughts of me bent over the table with him pounding into me from behind flittered through my brain. I shook them away.

Given the way he was blocking the door, I realized he wasn't going to let me leave the room until I agreed. "Fine, just food, okay?"

He grinned. "Just food. Come on. I know a good little spot."

Following him out the door, I was finally able to breathe. He'd stolen the air from my lungs, and I already knew he wanted to take much, much more.

We walked out into the brisk night together. I was hyperaware of him, his easy gait, his scent, the way his hands flexed to grip the door handle, the way he put his palm at my lower back and guided me down the stairs. I tried not to think about Claudia, about what she would say or how she would feel if she saw us together.

"I'll drive."

"No." I opened my car door and threw my backpack inside. "I'll go separate."

"Come on, now. At least let me drive you." He shoved his hands into his pockets and gave me the panty-melting smile I loved.

"No." I stayed strong though my knees were turning to jelly beneath me. "I'll go separate," I repeated with more force. "Where to?"

"Fine." He sighed and walked two spots down to his car before turning back to me. "Follow me. It's a bit of a hole in the wall. O'Flaherty's. You know it, yeah?"

"I think so. On the other side of the strip close to the thrift store?"

"That'll be the one. Drive safe, Laurel."

"You, too."

He watched as I closed my door and turned the ignition. Then he got into his car and I followed him across town to the Irish pub. His home turf.

I fretted the entire way, though keeping his brake lights ahead of me stopped me from running any red lights, as I worried about how Claudia would take such a betrayal. She talked about him incessantly. They'd only spent one night together, one I'd walked in on. And then he was on to his next conquest, and she was on to hers. Still, she kept talking about him as if he were the one, even as she bedded different men at least twice a week.

We pulled into the parking lot, Guinness signs glowing in the pub windows and people walking into the bar for a beer or two. I was too young to drink, but I could eat peanuts with the best of them.

I studied my reflection in the car mirror for a moment and tried to ignore the heat that thoughts of Eamon stirred in me. I needed to keep this short and get back home before anyone saw Eamon and me together and reported back to Claudia. That would be a disaster. All the same, I finger combed my hair and smoothed on some lip gloss.

I grabbed my wallet and left my purse and backpack in the car. Stepping onto the curb, Eamon was already waiting and took my elbow, leading me toward the door. The pub's rock music wafted into the night and a burst of laughter hinted at good times within.

His fingers were steady on my arm, gentle pressure leading where he wanted me to go. We entered the pub, the smell of fried food and beer on the air. A long bar stretched along the left hand wall and tables were scattered through the rest of the room. Two pool tables were in the back, men playing as women watched and drank. Eamon led me to a booth against the wall.

I sat and scooted in, expecting him to sit across from me. Instead, he peered down at me and ticked his chin up in a "move over" look. I moved against the wall and he slid in next to me. The room was suddenly warmer, my limbs heavier, my breaths conspicuous and loud. His thigh touched mine and I could have sworn there was some sort of an electrical jolt pulsing through me, sending a current to my clit.

A waitress, clad in a low cut tank top and shorty-shorts, walked up and smiled big at Eamon. His eyes were on me, not even looking at the abundant spill of cleavage the waitress was sporting.

"I'll have an O'Hara's. Laurel?"

"Coke, please." I smiled at the waitress who frowned back at me.

She hesitated, as if wanting to speak with Eamon, but he never even glanced in her direction. His eyes were on me the whole time. I blushed under his gaze. He seemed to relax into the booth further, letting his whole leg rest against mine. All muscle and strength.

After an exaggerated eye roll, the waitress walked away and returned with our drinks. She bent over and slid my drink to me, revealing her cleavage even more. Eamon slung his arm around my shoulders. I should have shrugged him off, especially given how Claudia felt about him. But I liked it, liked the feeling of being under his wing, even if it was selfish of me.

"Will that be all?" The waitress straightened, apparently giving up.

"No, I'll have Lou's special tonight. Make that two. You like burgers, love?" He asked me.

"I, um, sure. Yes."

"Yeah, so two of those, and bring some cheese sticks, please."

"Got it." She turned on her high heel and left.

Eamon squeezed my shoulder and clicked his glass into mine. "Cheers."

I sipped my drink as he took a long swig of his beer. He came away with a foam mustache, and I had the craziest impulse to lick it. I smiled and stifled my laugh.

"What?" He raised his eyebrows at me. "Something on my face, love?"

"No." I shook my head. "Not a thing?"

"Nothing?"

"Nope. Everything is totally normal."

He took another swig, even more foam collecting on his upper lip.

"How about now?"

I giggled. "Perfectly fine. I see nothing amiss."

He leaned in, the beer a mix of sweet and rich on his

breath. "Care for a taste?"

My heart leapt into my throat and I stared into his eyes, the blue even deeper in the dimness of the bar.

He pulled me closer, his fingertips pressing into my shoulder. Before I could back away, his mouth was on mine, his lips firm and warm. I clutched his shirt as he pushed me into the wall, caging me with his muscular body. My breath was gone, stolen by him as he licked along the seam of my lips, asking for entrance. He slid a hand down to my lower back and pulled me against him, pressing my breasts hard into his chest. I gasped at the friction on my nipples and he plunged his tongue into me.

I moaned into his mouth, and he growled a low response. His tongue mastered mine, and he eclipsed any thoughts I may have had about propriety or people watching. There was only him, his mouth, his body, the heat he stoked inside me. Opening my mouth wider, I gave him free rein over me. He gripped my hair, tilting my head back and kissing to my neck. My pussy was hot and wet, and I closed my eyes, imagining his wicked mouth between my thighs.

"God," I said on a heavy breath.

A thump sounded and I jumped. The waitress had plopped down a basket of cheese sticks, giving me the stink eye the entire time.

Eamon left a lingering kiss on my neck before straightening again and releasing me. He cut his gaze to the waitress and waved her away with an angry flick of his wrist.

I waited for him to apologize for being so … forward. But he only smiled and pulled me into his side again. He snagged a cheese stick and blew on it before putting it to my lips.

"Open, love." One side of his mouth quirked up in a devilish smirk.

"I can feed myself, you know." I couldn't stop the blush that ruled my cheeks.

"I know. Humor me?"

I opened my mouth hesitantly and he slid the tip in. I took a bite and the warm cheese and crispy crust melted on my tongue. He grinned and popped the rest of the cheese stick into his mouth.

He picked up another one, blew on it, and fed it to me in the same manner before finishing it off.

Being handfed by a handsome man was undeniably erotic. Something about the way he made sure it was cool enough for me to eat and then slid it between my lips. Somehow lewd but arousing all the same.

We polished off the cheese sticks as a new song began to play through the bar's sound system, a low bass beat thumping in my chest. Or was that my heart? Every time he looked at me, squeezed my shoulder, called me "love," my desire for him grew.

He allowed me to eat my burger on my own, thank goodness. Though he was attentive, making sure everything was to my liking as if he were the pub maître d'. We discussed his major and mine, how different they were, but both interesting. The waitress continued to eyeball me, but he still ignored her.

By the time we were finished, he was crowding me again, leaning in for another kiss. I wanted to give it to him, to let him have what he wanted. My eyes started to close as he ghosted his lips across mine and slid a hand up my thigh. His palm was hot, the warmth sinking through my jeans and heating my skin. I wanted his hands all over me. I melted into him as he kissed me. Though we'd just eaten, it was as if he'd become hungrier, holding me tight and growling like he wanted to devour me.

The pub door opened and I glanced to see a couple of acquaintances strolling in. The two girls were mutual friends with Claudia. *Fuck.*

I stiffened and pushed him away. "I have to go."

He furrowed his brow. "What, why?"

Chelsea spotted me and waved. She and Lydia made

their way over to us.

"Laurel, didn't know you did the pub thing." Lydia sneered. We'd never been close, and my heart sank with the realization that she'd likely text Claudia the first chance she got. I was screwed.

"I'm just… I was just hungry. So, Eamon offered—and so I—I mean we figured we'd get some dinner." For a languages major, I utterly failed at getting any coherent thought together.

Chelsea smiled warmly at me. "It's good to see you out and about instead of in the library. And who's your friend?"

"Eamon Wilson." He smiled.

Chelsea's smile faltered the slightest bit, no doubt recognizing his name and accent from Claudia's endless talk about him.

"Well, it's nice to meet you, Eamon. I'm Chelsea and this is Lydia. Would you mind if we joined you?"

I gripped his thigh. Though I liked Chelsea, I most certainly did not want to sit through the interrogation Lydia was likely cooking up.

"Sorry, ladies. We've already eaten and are ready to go our separate ways. Laurel was kind enough to help me with some translation work, so I bought her dinner in exchange." Eamon was trying to cover for me, but it didn't matter. Claudia would still blow her top once she heard I was with him at a pub.

He slid out of the booth and offered me his hand to help me up. I took it and got to my feet.

"I'm going to settle up." He strode to the bar.

"He's *that* Eamon, isn't he?" Chelsea whispered.

I nodded. "Could you two do me a favor and not tell Claudia?"

"I won't say a word." Chelsea squeezed my forearm.

Lydia gave me a too-sweet smile. "Me neither."

"Thanks, I appreciate it." I was a goner. Lydia was already digging in her purse for her phone. My hands went cold and I dreaded Claudia's tears and anger.

"You ready, lo—Laurel?" Eamon recovered quickly before calling me "love" in front of Chelsea and Lydia. It didn't matter. It was already a disaster.

"Sure. It was good to see you." I smiled weakly at Chelsea. "I'll catch you in class next week."

"See you then." Lydia had retrieved her phone and swiped across the screen, then looked at me as if waiting for me to leave so she could do her dirt.

Eamon took my arm and led me toward the door.

"Bye." Chelsea waved.

We walked into the chilly night air, and I hurried to my car.

Eamon leaned against my driver side door. "Where's the fire, love?"

I glared at him. "You know I have to get home and tell Claudia first before she hears it from Lydia. God, I should never have come out with you."

A flash of emotion flitted across his handsome face. I didn't want to think I'd hurt him, but I knew I had. I was messing everything up. I yanked my door handle, but it didn't budge with Eamon's large frame against it.

"Don't you worry about Claudia. In fact, I guarantee you she isn't at your dorm right this minute anyway."

"What?" I stopped my fruitless efforts at wrenching the door open.

"She's on a date. Noel. I know she likes accents, and Noel likes women. So, it's a perfect match." He moved so he stood in front of me, my back against the car door. "Now, come back to my dorm with me."

I stared up into his eyes and craned my head back against the top of the car door. He squeezed my hip and ran one hand into my hair, gripping me close to my scalp and pulling gently so my neck was exposed. He bent down and kissed my jugular. My knees went wobbly and I clutched his shirt.

"Please, Eamon. I can't." I was already begging. *I'm*

fucked.

"You can," he murmured against my throat and kissed to my ear. "Want to know what I'll do to you?"

A shudder of desire shot through me at his gravelly words. I was desperate to know. He licked the shell of my ear and pressed his body into me. His hard length rested against my stomach, and I imagined how tightly it would fit inside me. I nodded, and he pulled my hair harder.

"I'm going to eat your pussy like it's my favorite fucking dessert." He slid his hand around my stomach and down to my core. "Then I'm going to shove my cock into you, balls deep, and fuck you until you come all over me." He rubbed his fingers against my clit and bit my neck below my ear. "And then I'll keep fucking you as hard as I please until I shoot my load all over these lovely tits." He moved his hand from my hot pussy and squeezed my left breast, passing his thumb over my hard nipple in maddening strokes. "You'd like that, wouldn't you love?"

He bit my neck harder and I cried out. "Yes!"

"You want me to be rough with you, don't you?" His hips surged forward, his thick cock rubbing against my stomach. I wanted to wrap my hands around it, then my lips. "Tell me how you want it, love." He pushed his leg between my knees and lifted, my soaked pussy resting on his thigh as he created friction on my clit with small movements. "Tell me, Laurel." His voice was a growl.

"Hard." I was panting. "Rough. Take it from me."

He laughed, the sound low and sensual. "I will, love. Now get in my car. I'm not letting you out of my sight."

CHAPTER FOUR
EAMON

I KISSED HER AT every stop light between the pub and my place, and it was a fight to keep my hands off her as I drove. We snuck through the side entrance to the dorms, trying to avoid as many prying eyes and gossips as possible. I'd kept her hand in mine the entire way back to my place. I didn't want to break our contact, didn't want her to change her mind. She was quiet, though I felt her sneaking looks at me every so often.

At my door, I pulled the key from my pocket and opened it up. As planned, Noel was out, hopefully fucking Claudia senseless.

Laurel hesitated on the threshold. I turned to her and stroked my hand down her cheek. "Nothing will happen that you don't want."

She put her palm on my chest. "That's what I'm afraid of. There's so much that I want. Too much."

I thought I was randy. I thought I was turned on. I wasn't. When she said those words to me and looked up at me with her amber eyes, I wanted to eat her up, every last bit of her.

"Fuck me." I exhaled and yanked her into my room,

slamming the door behind us. I was all over her, ripping her jacket off before gripping her t-shirt and roughly pulling it up over her head. Her hands were on the hem of my t-shirt, but I was focused on her, getting her naked and tasting her. I palmed her tits. *Jesus.* Her nipples were stiff peaks beneath the lace. I bent down and took one in my mouth, teasing my tongue over her through the fabric.

She squirmed and moaned, but I slid one of my hands to her ass and gripped her hard, keeping her still, while I placed the other in her hair and pulled, forcing her to arch her perfect breasts to me. She dug her nails into my shoulder.

Her taste was heaven as I teased her tight nipple, running my teeth over her delectable flesh. I would have worshipped just her tits for hours, but my cock protested. It was time for her to be totally naked. I released her.

"Take the bra off." I popped the button on her jeans and pulled the zipper open as she reached behind her back. Slipping my hands down her waist and to her hips, I shucked her pants and panties off in one swift stroke. She stepped out of them and stood in front of me, naked and gorgeous.

I stared. Perfect teardrop tits, gentle curve to her waist, and a pretty pussy with blonde curls.

"You are fucking unbelievable, love."

She stared up at me, no fear in her eyes, as I perused her.

"I want to see you."

"You will." I advanced on her and pushed her back onto my bed. "Spread your legs."

I dropped to my knees and pulled my shirt over my head, tossing it away. She spread her knees and I got a glimpse of the sweetest pink I'd ever seen.

"More, love. Show it all to me." My cock was leaking like a son of a bitch, but I wasn't going to take her until I tasted her first.

She spread her knees wider. Her folds were glistening

and wet, the most gorgeous shade of light pink. My mouth watered. I reached up and put my hand on her chest, pushing her down. "Watch me."

I slid my hands under her ass and pulled her to the edge of the bed. She gazed down at me. When I exhaled along her dark pink clit, she shuddered.

"Eamon, please."

Her breathy voice was like a whip at my back, spurring me onward. I licked from her tight hole to her nub, and she jerked beneath me. Her honey taste was a delicacy on my tongue, and I wanted more. I wanted it all. I snaked my arm under her thigh and around so my forearm pressed on her lower stomach.

When I sank my tongue into her entrance, she moaned and her eyes rolled back. She was tight, her walls compressing my tongue as I fucked her. She dug her nails into my scalp as I moved up to her clit, swirling the tip of my tongue around it before laving it over and over, my tongue broad and flat against it.

I sank two fingers inside her as I kept working her with my mouth. She squealed at the sudden intrusion and tried to buck her hips. I pressed down harder with my forearm, making her take every bit of what I was giving. Her tight pussy gripped my fingers and I bore down even harder on her clit. I wanted her to come just from this before I fucked her proper.

I sped my tongue, no more teasing, and I matched my fingers to my tongue's stroke. Her breathing grew labored and she tensed around me, her thighs squeezing against my head, pressing me into her tender flesh the way I liked. I licked and shook my head against her.

"Eamon!" She froze, her hips no longer fighting me, and her pussy began to convulse around my fingers. "Oh my god."

Her moans lofted through the room and likely into the hall and down the corridor. I loved every sound, every coo that escaped her lips as I kept licking her and wringing her pleasure from her pussy. When she went limp, letting her legs fall open, I nibbled at her clit a little more, though she dug into my hair harder and tried to pull her hips away.

"Mine." I gave her one more licking kiss and pulled my mouth away. She stared up at me, her eyes glazed, her skin a rosy pink. Her rosy nipples were thick tips begging for my mouth.

My cock grew even harder. It was time. I hastily unfastened my jeans and stripped them and my boxers off.

Her eyes went to my cock and her mouth formed a pink 'O' when she saw it. Total ego boost.

I didn't want to spend another minute without my cock deep inside her, so I cut her appraisal short and crawled on top of her, pulling her up into the center of the bed.

Her tits jutted against me and I took one of her nipples in my mouth, her sweet taste on my tongue. I sucked and bit while kneading her other tit, until she was squirming and moaning. I moved back up and took her mouth. My cock rested against her wet pussy and I couldn't stop from thrusting lightly against her clit. She answered, lifting her hips to me and I groaned.

"Fuck, love." I said against her lips before thrusting my tongue inside her. She answered by wrapping her arms around my neck, pulling me even closer. Her tongue was slick velvet, stroking along mine. I bit her bottom lip and nibbled down to her neck before biting harder. She gasped and thrusted her hips even harder up to my cock.

I couldn't wait any longer. I had to claim her. I moved up to my elbows and grabbed a handful of her soft blonde hair in my right hand.

"I can't stop this, love. I'm going to fuck you hard, raw. The way you need."

"Yes." She sank her nails into my sides, the stings ricocheting through me and making my cock throb.

"Remember what I told you at the pub? How I'm going to come all over these tits?" I licked down her neck and bit down hard on her nipple. She arched beneath me as I positioned my tip at her entrance.

"Yes."

"Tell me you want this hard cock deep inside you. I want to hear it." I yanked her hair, pulling her head to the side and sucking on her neck.

"I-I want it hard. I want it deep. Please, Eamon."

Fuck, her begging was going to have me shooting my load all over her pussy before I even got inside.

"Then take it, love." I thrusted halfway home and she moaned, her voice bouncing off the wood paneled wall as I slid the rest of the way into her slick cunt.

CHAPTER FIVE
LAUREL

HIS COCK WAS SO thick and hard that a hint of pain mixed with the surge of pleasure as he entered me. He stilled once he was all the way, his tip hitting the back of me. My pussy convulsed around him, unused to the sudden intrusion, but sending skittering sparks of pleasure to my clit.

"Fuck, you're tight." He slid out and then back in again.

This time it was only pleasure. I ran my hands down his back as he drew out and shoved inside me again, roughly and with a groan. I loved it.

He let go of my hair and grabbed my wrists, pinning them to the bed on either side of my head. He leveraged up from me, bearing down on my hands as he started a hard rhythm, his thrusts jarring the bed, our skin slapping together.

"Look at me, love."

I stared into his blue eyes as he fucked me, my legs spread wide and my heels digging into his ass as his pistoned again and again into me. I'd be bruised and sore, but I wanted it all. His aggression was the hottest thing I'd ever seen. His broad chest flexed, the muscles drawn tight. His abs strained each time, the ridges becoming even more defined as he pounded me. My pussy was already tense again, his strokes going straight to my clit. I'd never been fucked hard before, not like this. I moaned at the sheer pleasure, the impacts against my pussy making every nerve ending on my body erupt.

I glanced down and watched his cock disappear into me and cursed. I wanted to touch him, to touch myself and feel him with my fingertips as he slid inside.

"Eyes on me, Laurel."

I stared at him, giving him what he wanted as he gave me everything I needed. I bit my lip and he growled before transferring my wrists into one of his hands. Then he reached down between us and placed his fingers along my mound, his thumb rubbing against my clit. I moaned and arched, pressing my tits into him for even more delicious friction.

"Like that?" he asked.

"Yes."

He increased the pressure of his thumb and pulled out and in with longer strokes. His head grazed my g-spot with each movement and my body began to tense again, the tide rising and the wave beginning to crest.

The side of his lips lifted in the slightest smile. "Your hot cunt is clamping down on me love, trying to get me to come. I won't. But when I'm ready, I'm going to paint your perfect tits white and then you're going to suck my cock clean."

His dirty words, delivered in the sexy Irish accent, sent me hurtling over the cliff.

"That's it." He grunted and slammed into me as I constricted around him, my orgasm swallowing me whole. I wanted to stay quiet, but he wouldn't let me, his thumb teasing my release out for longer as he hammered into me. I moaned my pleasure, long and low.

Awash in a sea of bliss, wave after wave of sensation

rocketed through me as he watched, his dark blue gaze taking in every expression on my face. I whimpered when my body relaxed again.

"That was the hottest shite I've ever witnessed, love," he said through gritted teeth.

I leaned up and kissed him, sated yet needing another taste. He answered, slowing his strokes and kissing me languidly. He released my wrists and broke our kiss, sitting back and lifting my hips to him.

He stared down at my tits as they bounced with each of his impacts. Gripping my hips, he pulled me into him over and over, his strokes becoming rougher. When he broke eye contact and looked at where our bodies joined, he let out a string of curses.

"I'm going to come, love. Squeeze your tits together."

I did as he said, putting my palms on the outsides of each of my breasts and pressing them together.

He groaned. "That's it."

He pulled out in one fast movement and straddled me as he furiously stroked his thick cock. I'd never seen an uncut one, and I was mesmerized by how the skin moved under his hand. I wondered what it would feel like in my mouth.

"Fuck," he yelled as he shot hot jets of come all over my tits, some of it splashing up to my chin. Every muscle on his body rippled with tension as he released, a deep growling rumble in his chest as he finished.

He moved off me, sitting on his knees at my side, and guided his cock to my mouth. "Get a taste, love. Clean it off."

I was eager to oblige, running my tongue along his head, the salty taste perfect on my tongue. I took him into my mouth as far as I could and licked up every bit of his spend left on his shaft. My mouth was still full of his cock when I swallowed.

"Oh, bless me." He stared down and moved his hips so that he was gently fucking my mouth. "I'm not ready for another round, but your mouth. Jesus Christ and all the saints."

I sucked harder, hollowing out my cheeks and smoothing my tongue up and down his shaft. His cock was still semi-hard and growing harder by the second. I wanted to make him come again. The thought of swallowing his seed had me bobbing my head back and forth as his hips sped up.

He leaned over me, putting his cock more squarely in my face with his body on one side of me and his hands propping him up on the other. I gripped his ass and dug my nails in, moaning as he pulsed further into me, his head grazing the back of my throat.

"Spread your legs and touch yourself."

I let one leg hang off the bed and lifted my hips to my fingers. I rubbed my wet clit, moaning on his cock at the overload of sensation.

"Fuck, Laurel. Fuck." His accent was more pronounced now, sounding more like "feck." I sank a finger inside myself and he thrust harder, his head hitting the back of my throat and making my eyes water. I wanted it all and wished I could swallow his entire length.

I drew my fingers out and pressed on my nub, rocking my hips up in the same rhythm he set as he fucked my mouth. My clit throbbed. Blood rushed to my nipples making them stand at attention again. I sucked and licked him, enjoying how he hardened in my mouth.

"I'm going to come again. Shite. Are you close?"

I nodded on his dick and he groaned. Strumming my clit faster, my hips jerked against my fingers. He increased his speed until I had to remain still and just let him use my mouth. His balls slapped into my cheek as he tensed even more.

I was there, and with a few more strokes, I came again, the waves surging through my pussy as I moaned around his cock.

"Swallow it, all of it." He grunted and hot seed filled

my mouth. I gulped it down, taking every last drop from him as my orgasm finally died down.

I stilled my hand, my clit aching, and he pulled his cock from my bruised lips.

He kissed my forehead. "You are a real corker, Laurel. Fucking hell. That was the hottest thing I've ever done."

I smiled up at him and he dropped a gentle kiss on my lips. He stepped over me and walked to the bathroom, gathering some tissue and cleaning me up before he lay down next to me.

Running his thumb over my lips, he asked, "Was that okay, love?"

"It was better than okay." *It was the best sex I'd ever had.*

He dropped onto his back and pulled me to his chest before whipping the blanket over us. I felt the particular ache between my legs. I'd been well loved and would likely be walking funny for a day or two. I wouldn't trade one second of it.

His strong arms wrapped around me. I was beat, but I couldn't stay the night. Thoughts of Claudia crept back in and worry gnawed at my stomach. Would Noel be enough for her or would she still rant and rage that I'd slept with Eamon?

"Don't worry. She's handled." Eamon, somehow sensing my thoughts, ran his hand through my hair.

"She's slept with other guys since you, you know? So I don't know if Noel can do the trick."

He shrugged and kissed the crown of my head. "I'm not worried."

"Because you don't have to live with her." I tried to pull away, though the thought of leaving him made me hurt in a way I didn't understand.

He flexed his arm. "You aren't going anywhere. Let's just sleep. I want to taste you again in the morning. Noel won't be back."

I flushed at his words and the promise of pleasure

inherent in them. But I tried to scoot away again. "I should get home in case—"

He chuckled. "You like to watch, love? You want to see Noel pound Claudia and listen to her squeals?"

"Ew, no. I don't want her to wonder where I am."

"She's far too happy right now to wonder about a damn thing. Now be quiet and let me hold you for a while."

Had I just been shushed? I opened my mouth to complain but he pulled me up to him in one easy movement and kissed me. His touch was gentle this time, but no less hot. He cupped the back of my neck and deepened the kiss before letting me go and scooting me down his chest.

"Go to sleep. It'll all be sorted tomorrow." He reached up and flicked off the lamp behind his bed.

Against my better judgment, I snuggled into his chest, relishing the feel of him. I'd wanted him for so long, this was like some sort of dream. I hoped it didn't end in disaster.

CHAPTER SIX
LAUREL

I WOKE TO AN intense screeching sound and then pain radiating through my scalp.

"What—" Eamon's voice rumbled but was cut short by the same shrill shriek.

My eyes adjusted and I realized Claudia had me by the hair and had dragged me from Eamon's bed. She was screaming bloody murder and drew back her hand to slap me. Eamon was on her in a second, gripping her wrist and wrenching her away from me. Noel dashed in the door, a bemused look in his face as he took in Eamon, a struggling Claudia, and a naked me. I ripped the blanket from the bed and covered myself before he could gawk for too long.

"Claudia, calm down you bloody harpy!" Eamon barked.

"You fucking bitch. You knew he was mine!" Claudia snarled at me, her small hands flexing into fists.

I wasn't concerned. I was more worried Eamon might hurt her because he had hell in his eyes and a strong grip on her.

"Oh, come on, you tart. You were on my dick and telling me I was your god not two hours ago." Noel

207

laughed and sat down on his bed. "You can't honestly be in here trying to claim this stiff prick is your man after all that."

Claudia struggled but got nowhere, her red hair mussed and her mascara running. "Just because I fuck other people doesn't mean I don't love him. He's been fucking other girls, too."

"In fact, I haven't."

Claudia stilled.

"Are you going to cool it?" Eamon asked. "I'll let you go. But if you make so much as a move in Laurel's direction, I'll throw you out. Understand?"

"Yes. Let me go." She was smiling, which made her seem even more crazed than when she was fighting and screaming.

The second Eamon released her, she turned to him and threw her arms around his neck. "I knew you loved me."

He didn't embrace her, just held his hands out next to him. His brow was furrowed and he shook his head. "No, I don't."

She tried to kiss him, but he backed away, giving all of us a full frontal view. He snatched his t-shirt from the floor and covered his cock, though the rest of his beautifully muscled body was on display.

"You do love me." Claudia tossed her hair over her shoulder and stepped toward him. "That's why you haven't slept with anyone else."

"No I stopped fucking other girls when I met Laurel." He looked over Claudia's head and caught my eye.

My heart expanded in my chest until I thought it would burst. *He'd stopped sleeping around for me?* I backed up and sank down onto his bed, pulling the blanket tight around me. This whole time I'd been crushing on him, he'd been doing the same to me?

"It's true." Noel leaned over and propped himself on his elbow before flashing me a too-bright smile. "No bitches since he saw you that one morning. I've only had to hear about it fifty times."

Eamon's cheeks reddened. I didn't think I'd ever seen him blush. "Shut your gob, Noel."

Claudia balled her fists but didn't move toward me. Instead of anger, hurt was in her eyes. Hurt I'd caused. My heart sank. Despite her current antics, she had always been a good friend to me.

"We are over." She shook her head. "Find yourself a new roommate, backstabber."

"Claudia, please—"

"I don't want to hear it!" Her scream was just as shrill as before and I had the impulse to cover my ears.

She turned on her heel and stalked from the room. Guilt wrenched my stomach in knots. I'd known how she felt about Eamon, but I'd slept with him anyway. I *was* a backstabber, just like she'd said.

Eamon walked over and knelt down in front of me.

"I'm gonna go down to the lounge." Noel popped up and left, closing the door behind him. I heard voices in the hall, no doubt other residents wondering what all the noise was about.

"Listen, love. You did nothing wrong."

I couldn't meet his gaze. "I think I did."

"I've never loved her. And it's obvious she doesn't love me, given her ways. It's only a passing fancy. Nothing more." He smoothed his palm along my cheek and dropped a kiss on my lips.

I pulled away. "I need to dress and leave. See if I can fix things with her."

"You don't have to—"

I stood and grabbed up my clothes before hurrying into the bathroom, blanket and all, and dressed. I came back out, not looking at Eamon, and glanced around for my bag. *Shit.* My things were in my car at the bar.

He'd thrown on some shorts and a jersey. "I can drive you to your car."

"No. I'll get someone downstairs to take me."

"Come on, Laurel. Let me at least drive you." He held out his hand to me.

I couldn't. Not after what had just happened. I shook my head, trying to ignore the burning tears that welled into my vision.

"Please?" He hadn't dropped his hand and his voice had a slight quaver, as if my refusal might crush him. He was so strong, so intense, that I couldn't believe his request was delivered with such vulnerability.

Instinctively, I reached out and took his hand. He smiled, the corners of his lips turning up just slightly, and led me out the door and down to his car. We rode to the pub in silence. I wrestled with how I could try and make it up to Claudia. Eamon sat quietly next to me, holding my hand but not intruding on my thoughts.

The pub's parking lot only had a few cars left from the night before. He pulled up next to my car and I opened my door to get out.

"Will I see you tonight?" He gripped my hand harder and pulled me to him. His lips met mine and took my breath away, just as surely as they did in this same parking lot the night before. I melted under his touch, his palm sweeping down my cheek and resting lightly at my throat. So much so, that I could get lost in this one moment. He tilted my head to the side and played his tongue along mine, teasing and stroking.

I pulled back before I was lost to him again. "I have to go. Claudia. I need to smooth things over."

"Tonight?" He asked again and stared at my lips like he wanted to take them again.

"I'll text you, okay?"

His face fell but he let go of my hand. "All right."

A twinge of pain shot through my chest at the thought that I'd hurt him. But I couldn't make any promises, not if I wanted to repair things with Claudia.

I dropped one more peck on his cheek and got out.

He waited until I was in my car and out on the road before he pulled out and headed back toward his dorm.

I pep-talked myself the entire way back to my dorm, pretending I was explaining the situation to Claudia and talking sense into her. I knew it wouldn't be that easy. With Claudia, it never was.

Her car was outside when I pulled up. After a few deep calming breaths, I climbed the steps to our room and crept down the hall. Listening at the door, I didn't hear anything, but I knew she had to be inside.

I eased the key into the lock and swung the door inward. She was lying on her bed, her back to me. She made no move to let me know she'd heard me, but I knew she did.

"Claudia, I'm sorry."

A sniffle.

I dropped my backpack and purse and went to her, sitting next to her on the bed. It was time to come clean. "I've had a thing for him ever since I saw him that morning."

"When he was with *me*." She laced her words with venom, but I heard the hurt, too.

I stroked her long red hair. This was classic Claudia – intense blowup and then she settled down into a gloom for a few days before she snapped back.

"Yes. I'm sorry. I shouldn't have. I got carried away." I let the guilt swirl around me.

"Do you love him?" She turned to look at me, her green eyes bloodshot in the morning light.

"I don't know." The answer sounded off even to my ears. *Did I love him?*

"Why doesn't he love me?"

I shook my head. There was no one who could answer that question. "Sometimes things just don't work."

"But you two work?" She turned away again.

I slid down in bed next to her, but didn't snug too close unless she went into blowup mode again. "I think we do. I think I want to give it more time. I think I want to try to be with him." I continued stroking her hair. "But I don't want to hurt you."

"Too late." Another sniffle.

"I know."

We lay in silence until she dozed off and started snoring lightly. I rose and covered her with her blanket before slipping into my own bed. It would blow over. I just had to wait it out. This wasn't our first blowup, but it certainly was our biggest.

It was Saturday, so we didn't have to worry about missing class. After our nap, we spent the rest of the day together, awkward at first, and then sort of making up as we went along. Me buying her dinner at her favorite restaurant went a long way to help. Her getting picked up at the bar by a Scottish grad student helped, too.

I purposefully ignored my phone. I wanted to give Claudia more time to heal, to forgive me, before I got in touch with Eamon again. A week, maybe. By that time, maybe she would have moved onto another guy. Even so, I longed to talk to him, to see him. When I closed my eyes, I saw the intense look on his face he'd had when he'd been inside me. Though I was repairing my relationship with Claudia, all I could think of was the man who'd torn us apart.

CHAPTER SEVEN
EAMON

"PULL YOURSELF TOGETHER, MATE." Noel opened the blinds in our dorm room and I blinked against the sun's harsh glare.

It was Wednesday. I'd skipped class, just like I'd done the two days before.

"Coach is going to ream your ass at practice." Noel's scolding had grown in intensity every day.

"I'm not going to practice." I drew my blanket over my head.

He ripped it off and tossed it across the room. "Get up. Rise and shine. You need a goddamn shower and a shave. Shake it off. She'll come back. And if she doesn't, her loss... Though, that's not true. I got a pretty good look at her that morning and damn. I would definitely do some filthy things to her sweet snatch." He whistled.

I was out of bed in a second, my hand wrapped around his throat. "Don't you fucking talk about her like that!"

"Better," he choked out.

I loosened my grip. What was I doing? Noel was my friend.

He grinned; his plan of taking the piss to get me moving clearly working.

"You're halfway to the shower. Keep on going." He made a show of pinching his nose.

"I don't stink."

"Sure. Sure. Tell it to the soap bar." He waved me into the bathroom. I dug my phone out of my shorts pocket. No messages, despite the fact I'd sent her countless texts and voicemails. The only thing that kept me from going to her dorm was Claudia. I didn't want to ruin her relationship with Laurel any more than I already had.

"Brush it off, mate. You can't just shut down because she's gone."

I slammed the bathroom door, closing off Noel's "voice of reason" routine.

I swiped across my phone. One more message. One more time.

Every morning when I wake up and realize you don't want me, my heart breaks all over again. ~E

I tossed my phone onto the counter and stepped into the shower.

CHAPTER EIGHT
LAUREL

THAT TEXT. I WAS sitting in my Wednesday morning Greek class, and I snuck a look at my phone. I couldn't take it any more. I'd stayed away from him for Claudia's sake. But now that she was already semi-serious with the Scot she'd picked up a few nights before, I refused to assuage her hurt feelings. Not after that text.

I closed my laptop and packed my backpack. The professor continued her lecture, though she raised an eyebrow at me. I never missed class. I shook my head, trying to assure her it wasn't an emergency. But it was.

I had to get to him. I hadn't slept well in days. I barely ate. He took up all my mental space, but I tried to stay strong for Claudia. Now, I didn't care if she never spoke to me again. I had to be with Eamon. I'd been a fool for waiting as long as I had.

I darted out of the room and down to my car. Traffic was light because it was in the middle of a session, so I made good time to his dorm. His car wasn't out front. *Shit.*

I sat for a moment in the parking lot and thought. I knew his schedule, for the most part, thanks to my and

Claudia's stalkerish ways. Wednesday was a practice day. I pulled out and drove the short distance to the soccer fields. I picked him out immediately, his tall, wide frame overpowering his teammates.

I parked and walked to the stands, choosing a seat along the bottom row. He wasn't looking in my direction. Instead, he was laser-focused on the ball, cutting in front of defenders, knocking two down, and pounding to the goal. At the last minute, he passed to Noel, who scored a goal.

The coach got in Eamon's face. He was yelling loud enough for the words to make it to my ears. "Do what we practiced. Respect the process. Cool your jets on the bench until you get your goddamn head in the game!"

Eamon trudged past the coach and was about to sit down on the bench when he spotted me, about twenty-five yards away. The second he saw me, it was as if a jolt electricity snaked between us, enough to tingle but not enough to sting. He didn't sit. Instead, he jumped the bench and charged toward me.

I stood and my heart warmed, and I couldn't believe I'd stayed away from him this long. He barreled over the running track and stopped just short of me.

"Eamon—"

"Shut up." He gripped my cheeks and kissed me, wrapping his arms around me and crushing me to his chest.

I slung my arms around his neck as he bent me back, taking my mouth and plundering it with his wicked tongue. I couldn't breathe, a haze of lust clouding what thoughts I had. I just wanted him. His scent enveloped me, sweat and his aftershave. My pussy grew wetter the more he expertly swirled his tongue around mine. He gripped my ass and pulled me to him, melding my body to his.

"Get a room, you wanker!" Noel called from the field. The rest of the team burst into laughter as Eamon straightened up and set me back on my feet.

The coach was standing on the sideline, hands on his hips. "Get the fuck out of here. No wonder you've been a dick for the past two practices."

Eamon smiled and took my hand, leading me back to the parking lot.

"Don't you have to, I don't know, finish—"

He whirled on me and kissed me again, taking me by surprise in the best way. After a few moments he broke the kiss and started toward the parking lot again.

"Anytime you say anything that will separate you from me, that's going to happen."

I smiled at his back as he pulled me along. "Really?"

"Try me, love."

"I think maybe you should stay and prac—"

He was on me in a split second. His lips were firm on mine, but he was smiling as he licked and bit at my lower lip.

"Now, come on. I want to welcome you back with a proper fucking."

My pussy tingled at his words and I dutifully followed him to his car. He sped back to his dorm, no lights to hold us up. He kept his hand on my thigh the whole way, playing his fingers back and forth, higher and higher each time.

I broke the silence, trying to cut the tension between us. "I feel like I should explain."

He whipped us around a corner. "No. I don't need an explanation. I need you to know if you ever go that long without contact again, I will find you wherever you are, and fuck you until you come so many times you pass out. Clear?"

"I-I… That's…"

"Love, I need you to understand that you're mine. I love you. I did from the moment I saw you. Tell me you're clear on that." He glanced over to me, his face drawn and serious.

"I love you, too." The words rolled off my tongue

217

easily, as if they were always meant to be there. I sat in shocked silence at myself.

He smiled, his eyes lighting up. "Much better. I think we're clear."

He screeched into a parking spot and pulled me into the dorm. We'd made it up the first flight of stairs before he pushed me against the wall and kissed me. He was rough, pulling my hair and biting down my neck. My panties were soaked and I wanted him inside me more than I'd ever wanted anything in my life.

He reached under my skirt, pushing it up and rubbing his fingers against me.

"So wet, love." Stroking back and forth over my clit, he drove me crazy as he licked and sucked my neck, his other hand in my hair keeping me still.

Pushing my panties aside, he sank a finger in me and I moaned, the sound carrying up the stairs above us.

"Fucking hell." He withdrew his fingers and released my hair, caging my neck instead. "Don't move. I'm going to fuck you right here against this wall."

He pulled his shorts down, revealing his hard length. He fisted himself and stroked my exposed clit with his tip.

"Oh my god," I tried to watch, but his hand at my throat tightened, his grip keeping my eyes on his.

Pleasure streaked through me, heightened by the knowledge that someone could catch us anytime, even in this side stairwell.

He pushed his head down to my entrance and gripped my thigh, spreading me open. "Ready, love?" He didn't wait for an answer and pushed inside me.

I squealed at the pressure and the delicious sensation of being filled. He drew back and sank all the way, pushing my ass against the wall as I arched my back.

"Pull your top down. Show me those luscious tits." His voice was gravelly as he started a punishing rhythm, the sounds of our skin slapping echoing all around us.

I opened my cardigan and pulled down my tank top

and bra.

He gazed down and licked his lips. Then he reached down to my ass with both hands and lifted me.

"Fuck, Eamon." He was so deep this way, my pussy open to him.

"Tight—little—cunt." He punctuated his words with thrusts as he sucked one of my taut nipples into his mouth. I moaned and clawed at his scalp.

His teeth played along the hard bud and he bit hard enough for me to cry out. My voice seemed to spur him on, because he pounded me harder and moved to my other nipple, biting down.

I moved one hand down between us and started rubbing my clit.

"Fuck me." He leaned away and watched me touch myself. Putting his hands beneath my knees, he spread me even farther open, using his arms to keep me against the wall.

"I'm going to come."

"Yes you are. Keep touching yourself like that. Hot as fuck." He stared as I pressed harder against my clit, then ran my fingers down to feel his cock sliding in and out of my slick pussy. I returned to my clit and stroked just right. My fingers combined with his thrusts had me falling over the edge.

"Eamon!" I bit my lip as my orgasm washed over me. My pussy spasmed on his cock, drawing him in deeper with each stroke. He put his forehead on mine and stared down to where he entered me again and again.

"I'm going to coat your pink pussy in me," he gritted out.

I was too lost in my own sensations, coming back down from the strongest orgasm I could remember. He slammed me a few more times and then pulled out, his cock hovering over my pink folds as he lashed my pussy with his seed. It was warm, mixing with my own wetness. He grunted as he shot the last burst onto me.

Kissing my lips, he gently set me down and rearranged my panties. "Don't even think of taking those off."

"Eamon. I can't go around with—"

"You will go around with your pussy covered in me. Oh, yes you will, love." He glared down at me, which excited me even more. "And you won't take these panties off until I decide to fuck you again." He stole another quick kiss. "Lucky for you, that will be soon."

EPILOGUE
LAUREL

Six Months Later

"DO I HAVE TO say 'blarney' a lot?"

Eamon laughed and squeezed my hand. We were whizzing through the streets of Dublin, far faster than seemed safe, in the back of a cab.

"I guarantee you if you say 'blarney' even once, my Da will think I brought home the village idiot of the Americas."

I frowned and snuggled into his side. "So what should I say then?"

"Whatever you American women say. Like 'nice to meet you, you silly Irish rube.' Something like that."

I giggled. "I'm sure that would make me plenty of fans."

"They are going to love you. Just like I do." He pulled my chin up to him and kissed me.

I ran my hand down his cheek to his shoulder, digging my nails in. He growled into my mouth and pulled me into his lap. His erection pressed into my ass.

"Look what you've done, love. We're about to meet my Mum and Da and you've gotten me all stiff in me

221

trousers."

I grinned. "Well, what are we going to do about that?"

He looked to the driver and kissed me hard again. "We're almost to the pub. You're in trouble."

He set me off his lap and adjusted himself in his pants. I was disappointed we didn't get to go any further, but the cab was sort of gross. We pulled up outside a real pub, music and banter streaming into the night. Eamon paid the cabbie and helped me out. We walked in and Eamon waved to a table full of people but pointed to the back. The older man at the table nodded and winked at me.

"Come on. Let's hit the loo. It was a long, hard trip, after all." He pulled me through the people milling about. It was a lively crowd and a band played in the loft above.

The hallway at the back was narrow and long, leading to two bathrooms. He pushed me into the women's room and chose the stall against the wall. I was so wet just contemplating what he would do to me.

"Hands on the wall, love. Bend over." He unbuckled his belt.

I kept facing him and kicked my chin up. "No."

"That's my girl." He grabbed my arm and whipped me around before grabbing the nape of my neck and forcing me to bend forward.

I reached out and braced myself on the wall. His fingers slid up my thighs and flipped my skirt up onto my lower back.

"No panties. Naughty little bit." He slapped my ass and then skimmed his fingers down to my pussy. "Wet, love?"

"Maybe a little."

He chuckled. "A lot. Just how I like it. Too bad I'm in a bit of a rush." He pushed his cock head against my entrance and I sighed as he entered me.

He withdrew and slid home again before gripping me

around the throat and pulling me up to him. He walked me forward so I was pinned against the wall as he surged in and out, slick sounds bouncing off the tile and back to my ears.

He held two fingers to my mouth. "Lick." I did as he'd said, running my tongue along his fingers. He withdrew them before I could capture them in my mouth. But then those fingers were on my clit and all I could think about was the pleasure he was giving me. He got right to business pressing and rubbing the way he knew I liked it.

The outer bathroom door creaked open and someone shuffled into the stall next to ours. I moaned low as I approached my climax, and Eamon slapped one hand across my mouth.

His palm pressed against my lips and the thought of someone hearing sent me over the edge and I came with a muffled cry. Eamon was in my ear whispering what a dirty girl I was when he grunted and came, his cock kicking and filling me as the person in the stall over flushed and exited the room quickly.

He withdrew his hand and his cock, straightening his pants as I hastily cleaned up.

"Lipstick?" I asked him.

He smirked, licked his thumb, and wiped at the corner of my lip. "Perfect now. Though I must say when you look all mussed is my favorite."

"Of course it is, bad boy." He swatted my ass as we washed up and headed back out to meet his family.

Our quickie seemed to have soothed the few nerves I was feeling, and Eamon's warm palm encompassing mine made everything feel right. He led me to the rowdiest table in the pub. They stopped talking and looked up at us, smiles lighting their faces. The man and woman situated at the closest end stood and embraced Eamon before looking me over.

"And who's this lovely betty?" Eamon's Da asked.

He took one of my hands and the older woman,

Eamon's Mum, took my other.

Eamon beamed with pride. "Mum, Da, this is Laurel, my fiancée."

Dark Romance by Celia Aaron

COUNSELLOR
The Acquisition Series, Book 1

In the heart of Louisiana, the most powerful people in the South live behind elegant gates, mossy trees, and pleasant masks. Once every ten years, the pretense falls away and a tournament is held to determine who will rule them. The Acquisition is a crucible for the Southern nobility, a love letter written to a time when barbarism was enshrined as law.

Now, Sinclair Vinemont is in the running to claim the prize. There is only one way to win, and he has the key to do it—Stella Rousseau, his Acquisition. To save her father, Stella has agreed to become Sinclair's slave for one year. Though she is at the mercy of the cold, treacherous Vinemont, Stella will not go willingly into darkness.

As Sinclair and Stella battle against each other and the clock, only one thing is certain: The Acquisition always ends in blood.

MAGNATE
The Acquisition Series, Book 2

Lucius Vinemont has spirited me away to a world of sugar cane and sun. There is nothing he cannot give me on his lavish Cuban plantation. Each gift seduces me, each touch seals my fate. There is no more talk of depraved competitions or his older brother – the one who'd stolen me, claimed me, and made me feel things I never should have. Even as Lucius works to make me forget Sinclair, my thoughts stray back to him, to the dark blue eyes that haunt my sweetest dreams and bitterest nightmares. Just like every dream, this one must end. Christmas will soon be here, and with it, the second trial of the Acquisition.

SOVEREIGN
The Acquisition Series, Book 3

The Acquisition has ruled my life, ruled my every waking moment since Sinclair Vinemont first showed up at my house offering an infernal bargain to save my father's life. Now I know the stakes. The charade is at an end, and Sinclair has far more to lose than I ever did. But this knowledge hasn't strengthened me. Instead, each revelation breaks me down until nothing is left but my fight and my rage. As I struggle to survive, only one question remains. How far will I go to save those I love and burn the Acquisition to the ground?

Romantic Sports Comedy
by Celia Aaron & Sloane Howell

Cleat Chaser

Kyrie Kent hates baseball. She hates players even more. When her best friend drags her to a Ravens game, she spends the innings reading a book... Until she gets a glimpse of the closer—a pitcher who draws her like a magnet. Fighting her attraction to Easton Holliday is easy. All she has to do is keep her distance, avoid the ballpark, and keep her head down. At least, all that would have worked, but Easton doesn't intend to let Kyrie walk so easily. When another player vies for Kyrie's attention, Easton will swing for the fences. But will Kyrie strike him out or let him steal home?

Short, Sexy Reads by Celia Aaron

Forced by the Kingpin
Forced Series, Book 1

I've been on the trail of the local mob kingpin for months. I know his haunts, habits, and vices. The only thing I didn't know was how obsessed he was with me. Now, caught in his trap, I'm about to find out how far he and his local cop-on-the-take will go to keep me silent.

Forced by the Professor
Forced Series, Book 2

I've been in Professor Stevens' class for a semester. He's brilliant, severe, and hot as hell. I haven't been particularly attentive, prepared, or timely, but he hasn't said anything to me about it. I figure he must not mind and intends to let me slide. At least I thought that was the case until he told me to stay after class today. Maybe he'll let me off with a warning?

Forced by the Hitmen
Forced Series, Book 3

I stayed out of my father's business. His dirty money never mattered to me, so long as my trust fund was full of it. But now I've been kidnapped by his enemies and stuffed in a bag. The rough men who took me have promised to hurt me if I make a sound or try to run. I know, deep down, they are going to hurt me no matter what I do. Now I'm cuffed to their bed. Will I ever see the light of day again?

Forced by the Stepbrother
Forced Series, Book 4

Dancing for strange men was the biggest turn on I'd ever known. Until I met him. He was able to control me, make me hot, make me need him, with nothing more than a look. But he was a fantasy. Just another client who worked me up and paid my bills. Until he found me, the real me. Now, he's backed me into a corner. His threats and promises, darkly whispered in tones of sex and violence, have bound me surer than the cruelest ropes. At first I was unsure, but now I know – him being my stepbrother is the least of my worries.

Forced by the Quarterback
Forced Series, Book 5

For three years, I'd lusted after Jericho, my brother's best friend and quarterback of our college football team. He's never paid me any attention, considering me nothing more than a little sister he never had. Now, I'm starting freshman year and I'm sharing a suite with my brother. Jericho is over all the time, but he'll never see me as anything other than the shy girl he met three years ago. But that's not who I am. Not really. To get over Jericho – and to finally get off – I've arranged a meeting with HardcoreDom. If I can't have Jericho, I'll give myself to a man who will master me, force me, and dominate me the way I desperately need.

***

Zeus
Taken by Olympus, Book 1

One minute I'm looking after an injured gelding, the next I'm tied to a luxurious bed. I never believed in fairy tales, never gave a second thought to myths. Now that I've been kidnapped by a man with golden eyes and a body that makes my mouth water, I'm not sure what I believe anymore. . . But I know what I want.

<u>About the Author</u>

Celia Aaron is the self-publishing pseudonym of a published romance and erotica author. She loves to write stories with hot heroes and heroines that are twisty and often dark. Thanks for reading.

20853693R00132

Printed in Great Britain
by Amazon